MW01258128

TAKE YOU

(A Rylie Wolf FBI Suspense Thriller—Book 5)

Molly Black

Molly Black

Bestselling author Molly Black is author of the MAYA GRAY FBI suspense thriller series, comprising nine books (and counting); of the RYLIE WOLF FBI suspense thriller series, comprising six books (and counting); of the TAYLOR SAGE FBI suspense thriller series, comprising six books (and counting); and of the KATIE WINTER FBI suspense thriller series, comprising eleven books (and counting).

An avid reader and lifelong fan of the mystery and thriller genres, Molly loves to hear from you, so please feel free to visit www.mollyblackauthor.com to learn more and stay in touch.

Copyright © 2022 by Molly Black. All rights reserved. Except as permitted under the U.S. Copyright Act of 1976, no part of this publication may be reproduced, distributed or transmitted in any form or by any means, or stored in a database or retrieval system, without the prior permission of the author. This ebook is licensed for your personal enjoyment only. This ebook may not be re-sold or given away to other people. If you would like to share this book with another person, please purchase an additional copy for each recipient. If you're reading this book and did not purchase it, or it was not purchased for your use only, then please return it and purchase your own copy. Thank you for respecting the hard work of this author. This is a work of fiction. Names, characters, businesses, organizations, places, events, and incidents either are the product of the author's imagination or are used fictionally. Any resemblance to actual persons, living or dead, is entirely coincidental. Jacket image Copyright Robsonphoto, used under license from Shutterstock.com.
ISBN: 978-1-0943-3004-4

BOOKS BY MOLLY BLACK

MAYA GRAY MYSTERY SERIES
GIRL ONE: MURDER (Book #1)
GIRL TWO: TAKEN (Book #2)
GIRL THREE: TRAPPED (Book #3)
GIRL FOUR: LURED (Book #4)
GIRL FIVE: BOUND (Book #5)
GIRL SIX: FORSAKEN (Book #6)
GIRL SEVEN: CRAVED (Book #7)
GIRL EIGHT: HUNTED (Book #8)
GIRL NINE: GONE (Book #9)

RYLIE WOLF FBI SUSPENSE THRILLER
FOUND YOU (Book #1)
CAUGHT YOU (Book #2)
SEE YOU (Book #3)
WANT YOU (Book #4)
TAKE YOU (Book #5)
DARE YOU (Book #6)

TAYLOR SAGE FBI SUSPENSE THRILLER
DON'T LOOK (Book #1)
DON'T BREATHE (Book #2)
DON'T RUN (Book #3)
DON'T FLINCH (Book #4)
DON'T REMEMBER (Book #5)
DON'T TELL (Book #6)

KATIE WINTER FBI SUSPENSE THRILLER
SAVE ME (Book #1)
REACH ME (Book #2)
HIDE ME (Book #3)
BELIEVE ME (Book #4)
HELP ME (Book #5)
FORGET ME (Book #6)
HOLD ME (Book #7)
PROTECT ME (Book #8)

PROLOGUE

Nights were always the worst.

Ever since Lance had left, Marie Bottoms had a hard time falling asleep. Everything seemed so quiet, like it was her against the world.

Sixteen days. That was how long he'd been gone. But more importantly, sixteen nights. Sixteen sleepless nights, spent with her heart in her throat and her comforter pulled up over her head like some frightened child.

She'd spent most of the day fulfilling orders, threading silver beads onto elastic cord to make her custom creations. It kept her busy, kept her mind from wandering to what he was up to. Now, she looked down at her phone for the thousandth time that day, hoping for a text from her husband. He used to do those things so incessantly, she'd almost been annoyed by it. Just a, *Hey, checking in* or a *U ok?* or a *Thinking about you.* Or even just something to let her know she was on his mind.

But she wasn't, anymore, was she?

She stood up from the couch, leaving the television on because it kept her company. Poor company, even though she'd always found the announcer's voice comforting and his jokes funny. Taking her empty teacup to the sink, she decided to leave it there until morning. If she could get to bed right away, the Sleepy-time tea could sometimes lull her off before she had a chance to obsess about what had gone wrong in her life, leading her to this horrible, desperate loneliness.

She checked the back door to make sure it was locked, something Lance had always done for them. He'd always been so concerned about the safety of their little family. That was one of the things she'd liked most about him. He was careful. So steady, responsible, and well, predictable.

That was, until Carrie.

His secretary.

Marie noticed something was wrong, almost the same time the eighteen-year-old bombshell from Florida had started working for Lance's firm. One moment, it was, "our old admin's retiring, hope we can find someone to replace her," and the next, he was staying late. Arranging long, out of town business trips. Forgetting to call or text her during the day to check in. Coming home, smelling heavily of flowery perfume.

And then, one day, just over two weeks ago, he hadn't come home at all.

She'd gotten a text, of all things, explaining how it was. He said he was sorry, but he wouldn't be coming back to their house, ever. He wanted a divorce, but he'd keep her in the house, make sure she was taken care of. He apologized that it hadn't worked out.

Now, she looked down at her phone and saw it, silent. She hadn't had any communication from him at all in over three days.

Marie laughed bitterly at that, as she locked the front door, set the alarm system, double-checked it, and went upstairs to brush her teeth. As far as she'd known, it *was* working out. He had a good job, she had a thriving shop on Etsy, selling fancy cellphone charms, and they were trying to start a family. She'd even told him she was going off birth control last month, and he'd been excited about that.

Now, she was alone. Twenty-six-years-old, and about to be divorced.

When she was finished getting ready in the bathroom, she left the light on there, closing the door only partway before plugging in her phone to charge and jumping into her big, lonely bed.

She lay there for a moment, staring at the ceiling, watching the shadows of trees swaying in the moonlight cast through the window. Faraway, a television announcer said something, and the audience roared with laughter.

Did she lock the back door?

She couldn't remember. Marie had always had OCD tendencies, which was why she let Lance take care of all that. If she was in charge of it, she'd constantly obsess about whether it was done, and would check and re-check things to near madness. That had always been her problem; she never trusted herself. She'd been so happy when she'd found him, someone she could trust, to take care of everything and make sure she was safe.

Her lips curled into a snarl and she threw the covers off, surprised at how cold it'd become in such a short period of time. Shivering, she rushed down the steps to see Jimmy interviewing some sports star she didn't recognize. She checked the back door.

Locked.

She groaned at herself. *Of course it was locked, stupid. You always second-guess yourself.*

And she'd been doing it more and more in the last few weeks. Questioning herself, her sanity. She hated to think that it was that man, her cheating husband, who'd given her all her confidence, but it was true. Now, she felt adrift.

But what was she, a child? Needing someone to guide her through life? No, she had her own business. She was a fully independent adult. She'd survived without Lance Bottoms for eighteen years, and she could do it again. She could do this.

Turning, she went to the television and switched it off. *Adults are happy with their own company,* she told herself, smiling in triumph.

She marched to the front door and put her hand on the banister, ready to climb the steps and fall into her bed, when she noticed the security system panel on the wall near the front door.

A light on it was blinking.

Had it ever done that before? She couldn't remember. Lance had managed all that. He was a techno-geek, and it had been his fun toy— he knew all the ins and outs of it, what every little button on it did.

She moved closer to it and saw that the blinking was next to the words, "BACK DOOR." Another word was flashing on the panel, too, right next to it. UNLOCKED.

That was strange. Hadn't she just checked that?

Probably a malfunction. It had done that a few times, when Lance was here. She pressed a button, hoping to turn it off. It didn't work.

She tried a couple more, but none of them seemed to do anything, either. "Stupid thing," she said, smacking it and half-wishing it was Lance's face. "You're broken."

Then she went through the house, once again, to the back door. Maybe she'd disturbed some sort of sensor, sent it off track, and she just needed to flip a switch.

She went to the door, looking for the wiring, but she noticed something else.

The back door was no longer locked. It was closed, but the lock had not been engaged.

This time, though, she was sure she *had* engaged it. She remembered twisting it. Had she not twisted it hard enough? No, she was certain she had.

3

I'm going crazy. Without Lance here, I'm losing it.

Then, she thought she heard a noise, outside, on the back deck. A crack. Like a foot stepping on a dried branch. But nearby, almost right by the door.

Pulling open the door, she slowly, cautiously, poked her head out.

All was quiet. Her house backed up to tall trees, and a little creek. She could hear the burbling of its waters, the slight rustle of the leaves, the lone cry of a hawk in the trees above. But nothing else. Reaching for the switch on the wall behind her, she flipped on the back light, illuminating the small patch of deck. Nothing.

I am so paranoid. I've got to loosen up, she thought, rubbing her eyes.

But the second she regained her focus, the man was there. Standing in front of her.

Marie froze in terror, recognition sparking within her. She couldn't remember where she'd seen him; all she knew was that he didn't belong here, on her back deck. She scrambled back a few steps, hitting the door and tripping over the transom as she frantically tried to remember where she'd left her cell phone.

Upstairs. On the charger. A lot of good it's doing you, now.

Before she could try to stand, he reached for a pillow from the couch and stood over her. He brought it down over her face, holding tight there. She flailed her arms, trying to escape, but it was no use. She was already half out of breath from the fright, so she quickly went dizzy from lack of oxygen. Her lungs burned, so hot she thought they might explode, until it felt like they did. Then, gradually, everything went numb, and she could feel no more.

CHAPTER ONE

Bang. Bang. Bang.

Shooting pain spiraled stars into Rylie Wolf's vision as she stood in front of a blank wall in her apartment. She opened her mouth and let out a silent scream, punctuating it with the perfect word:

"Dammit!"

Rylie clutched her thumb as the fireworks of pain whizzed up to her elbow. She dropped the hammer, which fell on her foot. She screamed louder, then hopped around her apartment, clenching her teeth at the pain before pulling a chair out from the kitchen set and sinking down into it.

She hated this apartment. This dull, drab, old, cruddy apartment.

She looked around sourly. The place had come courtesy of the federal government, when they'd started the new field office out here in Rapid City, South Dakota. She'd heard plenty of stories about government overspending, but apparently, whoever'd decided on this place for her and the other agents in the Rapid City FBI office had missed the memo. It was a one-bedroom crap-hole in what looked like a rectangular brick prison, 1970s construction, across from a fast-food restaurant and a gas station.

It smelled. Nothing worked. It took forever to get hot water in the shower. *Forever.* Sometimes she'd turn on the faucet, go and heat up a frozen meal for dinner, and come back, and it *still* wouldn't be warm.

It hadn't mattered much, at first. She was so busy on cases along highway 86 that she was barely home. And Rylie had never been one to enjoy HGTV or home decorating magazines. But the past week, after closing out a case in Montana, she'd been back here, and gradually getting more annoyed by her surroundings.

Also, more antsy.

She thought that adding some nice artwork to the walls she'd freshly painted might help.

But now, as she looked at her swelling, purple fingernail, she realized she was going to need a lot more help than that.

Taking a swig of her beer, she looked over at the nail she'd barely managed to hammer into the wall. She'd measured to make sure it was exactly in the center, but now, it looked kind of . . . off.

She sighed down at the painting of the Seattle coast she'd brought with her. As bad as the experience was that had forced her to leave Seattle, she still had a soft spot for it. She'd moved out there for college, and had always considered it home—definitely more of a home than the place she lived with her father in Wyoming. She thought the painting would brighten the drab place up, make her happier. It wasn't working. Now, she felt so far away from it, she wondered if she'd ever get back.

Drumming her hands on the table, she looked over at her phone again. No calls.

It wasn't just the décor that had her antsy, or that her boss, Kit, hadn't put her and her partner, Michael Brisbane, on anything exciting in over a week. It had everything to do with what she'd found at Elephant Hole, the military outpost in Montana.

All it takes is one little piece of evidence. It might be everything. The thing that cracks the case wide open.

That is what her partner had said when she'd found the piece of the rear-view mirror from a car, dusty and broken at the bottom of a dried well. They'd been led there by another piece of evidence-- a necklace her sister Maren had worn. She'd thought she'd seen a fingerprint on it, and sent it to be analyzed.

And now she was waiting. Waiting to find out if the newest piece of evidence would finally bring her some peace of mind as to what had happened to her sister, almost twenty years ago.

Had she been kidnapped, and by whom? That question had plagued Rylie, ever since she was a child, when she found her mother, best friend, and her best friend's mother, murdered at a campsite along the Montana-Wyoming border. After that horrific day at Story Creek, Maren, her older sister, had been declared missing, and there had been no leads, since.

It was the driving force behind why Rylie had wanted to become an FBI agent in the first place. She'd always, in her heart of hearts, hoped that she could bring some closure to herself and her estranged father, who'd suffered just as much as she had.

6

As she sat there, sucking on her swelling thumb, the phone rang. The number was from headquarters. She sucked in a breath and answered. "Rylie Wolf."

"Hey, Ry, it's Marsden."

Marsden, lead forensics analyst. She wasted no time with small talk. "Yeah, hey, so you're calling about the mirror? What'd you find out?"

"We were able to extract the fingerprint, and ran it through our database. We got a positive match."

She straightened. It sounded too good to be true. After all the setbacks, they actually had an ID of a person of interest, someone who had been in the same place where Rylie's sister had been. "Yeah?"

"Yeah, but . . . "

Of course, there had to be a "but." Nothing could ever be easy. "Is he dead?"

"No, actually. The guy's name is Griffin Franklin, and he's in prison right now for another murder."

Another murder. Of course. The person who'd done that to Maren wouldn't be a preschool teacher. The man was a killer. This was looking better and better. Rylie didn't want to get her hopes up, but here was a man who'd been in the same place as her sister, and had a history of violent crime. It was the best lead they'd had in, well . . . forever.

"Another murder? That's not a but. Why is that a but?"

"Well," Marsden said, clearing his throat. "It's going to be a bear if you want to get in there and interview him. He's killed several women, and he's in maximum security at North Dakota Correctional Center now because of his violent tendencies."

She didn't care. This was a small obstacle to overcome in comparison to the mountain she'd just climbed. "I'll get access."

"Good luck with that," Marsden said, doubtful.

"Thanks," she said, ending the call. She didn't have room in her life for doubt, now. As far as she was concerned, it was full speed ahead. She quickly dialed Kit, then jumped up, pacing the living room, her aching toe forgotten.

When her supervisor answered, it was with the same, no-nonsense greeting Rylie appreciated. The woman was stern, but fair and efficient, unlike her old supervisor in Seattle, Bill Matthews, who had shipped her off here just because she was a bit outspoken and irreverent. Rylie got along with Kit, at least. "Kit, here."

"Hi, Kit, it's Rylie," she said.

Kit sighed. "Nothing new. Didn't I say I'd call you if I had something for you?"

Rylie laughed. She'd been calling Kit almost every day, hoping for a new case to sink her teeth into. Instead, she and Michael had been forced to work on some dull clean-up work on a solved case in town, amassing interviews. "Yes, I know, but—"

"Have you finished those interviews?"

"Yes, all of them, but—"

"I didn't see the reports come across my desk."

Rylie groaned. If there was anything she hated about the job, it was writing the reports. She'd tried to pawn them off on Michael, but he'd refused. So she just had to sit behind her computer and get them done. Torture.

"I'm working on it, but I had another question for you."

"Shoot."

"I need to get into North Dakota Correctional Center's maximum security unit. I need to conduct an interview there. Can you help get me a pass?"

There was a pause. "What prisoner? This isn't for—"

"It's for an old case, and I have a little hunch about it. I wanted to check it out."

"That could be tough," she said. "What's the prisoner's name?"

"Griffin Franklin."

"Griffin . . ." she murmured. She was probably writing it down. "I know him. He's a big problem. Killed all those women in North Dakota. He's going to be a challenge."

"Yes, I know, but—"

"The best I can do is put in for it. And we'll see. Might take some time, if they allow it at all."

She smiled. "Yep, that's all I'm asking. Thanks so much."

"Not a problem. Now . . . those reports?"

"Working on them," she muttered.

She ended the call and tapped her fingers on the kitchen table. Then she opened her laptop, and did a quick Google search on the infamous Griffin Franklin.

A number of results popped up. The first article's headline caught her eye: *FRANKLIN SENTENCED TO 6 LIFE SENTENCES FOR MURDERS*

She scanned down to the photograph of an older man in a jumpsuit, his hands tied behind his back. He was balding, and had tattoos up his neck, and a face with a very flat jaw. He looked kind of like a frog. The scowl on his face was frighteningly cold.

The crackle of thunder outside thrust her into the memory of her hiding in that spot in the RV, trying to make herself as small as possible so they wouldn't find her. The sound of gunshots, each one making her stifle a gasp. Three shots, altogether.

Voices, then. Male. "I thought there were three?" one had said.

"Naw. Just those two."

And then the door had slammed, and after that, nothing.

Nothing for hours and hours. Or at least, it seemed like that. Rylie had been bathed in sweat by the time she'd pulled herself out from her hiding spot. She'd crept to the dirt-crusted window over the RV's kitchenette sink and stared out at the bodies, lying motionless in a circle. Kiki, Rose, and her mother. They'd all been shot, once, in the head.

But no Maren. Maren was gone.

She hadn't seen either of the men. Was one of them this man, Griffin Franklin? She wished she'd been brave enough to peek out. Maybe then she'd have something to go on. But as far as she could remember, she had no memory of ever having seen them at all.

But the things the men outside had said meant something, had made Rylie think that this wasn't just random. That the men—maybe this Griffin Franklin—knew them. Had followed them. Had maybe even interacted with her family before.

She read the article:

On Tuesday, a North Dakota judge sentenced Griffin Franklin to serve six consecutive life terms in prison, one for each of his victims, without the possibility of parole, in what police say was one of the most horrific crimes the state has ever seen.

After overwhelming evidence was presented, the jury easily found Franklin guilty of killing six women across the state over the course of a ten-year period.

South Central District Judge Morris Hastings handed down Franklin's sentence to serve the rest of his life in prison, but before hearing the judge read the verdicts, Franklin addressed the court, saying, "I can honestly tell you that I'm not a bad man, and I am at peace with the knowledge that I am innocent of these crimes."

One of Franklin's lawyers asked the judge to consider the possibility of parole when considering his sentence. However, prosecutor Max Smith said Franklin is a danger to the community and has shown no remorse for his crimes.

North Dakota doesn't have the death penalty.

She read the man's statement, over and over again. *I am innocent of these crimes.*

Rylie had met a lot of criminals in her time, and she'd found that to be the true mark of a total sicko—believing and professing in one's innocence, even when the jig was up.

Then she Googled his history, trying to find out where he'd lived twenty years ago. At first, she had no luck. But then she found an address for him, from about fifteen years ago.

Long Butte, Wyoming.

Not very far from Story Creek, where the murders had occurred.

Googling some more, she came across photos of him as a younger man, when he'd had scruffy brown hair. He was skinnier, but still a large man, with the same, dead eyes and scowl. Still, it struck no chord within her. He was a stranger.

But that didn't mean he was innocent.

She stared at the photograph. Did he know what happened to Maren?

Now, Rylie was determined to find out. She'd get that approval if it was the last thing she did. But until then . . .

If there was someone who might remember if this man, Griffin Franklin, had been around or noticed her family all those years ago, she knew exactly who to ask.

CHAPTER TWO

Rylie pulled into the old apartment complex in Cody, Wyoming, next to her father's red Ford Ranger. It hadn't moved since the last time she'd been there, and was parked perfectly in the spot, with almost military precision. Her father was neat, that way.

The apartment complex was a two-story building with brown paneled walls and mustard-colored doors. Modern, probably, about thirty years ago. But now, it looked as if it'd definitely seen better days. The paint was peeling on most of the doors and there were grills, bicycles, sporting equipment, and unsightly lawn chairs on the balconies. The last time she'd come here, she knew her father's place at once, because his balcony was the only one that was absolutely spotless. That was her dad.

They had never seen eye-to-eye. Not even before her mother was murdered. Her father had always been close-lipped, quiet. He'd completely withdrawn, after her mother's murder, leaving Rylie to be raised essentially by Hal, the old rancher next door.

But gradually, she hoped that they could bridge the distance.

She climbed the stairs and went to the door, thinking her visit would have to be better than last time. Last time, the conversation was stilted and painful, even with her partner, Michael there to help lighten the mood.

Rick Wolf was just as handsome as ever, tall, with his dark hair and piercing blue eyes. There was more salt than pepper in his beard, now, and his belly filled out his trademark flannel shirt more fully. There were more trademark scars of his heavy drinking there, too—his eyes were bleary and his face, bloated, with broken blood vessels dotting his nose. Again, he looked utterly mystified at her appearance.

"Rylie," he said stiffly. "Back again? You really are not staying away."

She forced a smile. "That's right. Trying to be here for you." She lifted a bag of fried chicken. "Brought lunch!"

He swallowed and looked at the bag. "I already ate." But he pushed open the door anyway, and let her through.

11

"All right," she said, going into the kitchen and setting the bag down. "Then we can talk while I eat. You have plates?"

He motioned to the cabinet right behind her head. "I don't eat out of a trough."

She pulled two down, just in case he changed his mind, and dug into the bag for the bucket of chicken.

"You want something to drink?" he asked her as he joined her there. "I've got a few Cokes, and –"

"Coke is great," she said, watching as he opened the fridge. It was stocked with soda. No beer. So he was staying on the wagon. That was good.

She opened the can and took a sip as she sat down with her plate of chicken and potatoes. "So, what's going on around here?"

He shrugged. "It's Cody. Nothing goes on around here, Rylie. That's why I like it."

She smiled. She couldn't blame him. After what had happened to their family, he only wanted to be left alone. That's why she was left to be cared for by Hal Buxton, and escaped to Seattle for college as fast as she could. He wanted to tune absolutely everything and everyone out.

"I guess that's good."

But the same thing couldn't be said for Rylie. Where her father had run away from the action, Rylie had run toward it, applying for the FBI almost the second she graduated from college. He watched her take a bite of chicken, the greasy fried skin hanging from her mouth, and said, "I'm sure the same can't be said for you. You working on that case still?"

She shook her head. "That one got put to bed. I have another case I'm working on in Rapid City, but it's boring. Interviews and stuff."

He frowned. "Boring . . . you mean, not dangerous?"

"Everything *can be* dangerous, Dad. You can be struck by lightning, sitting in your recliner."

He shook his head. "I don't know why you do it. What you get out of it. Most women your age are settled down and married now."

She knew that. She was in her mid-thirties and though she didn't keep in touch with any of the girls from college, she assumed most of them were married with kids, now. It wasn't that she didn't want a family. She'd dated, thinking it would happen eventually. At first, she'd told herself she had time. Now, that time was dwindling. She nodded.

"What about that fella you brought over?"

He meant Michael Brisbane. "He's my partner," she reminded him. She'd told him that many times during their short visit, but apparently, he'd forgotten. "That's all."

"Doesn't have to be all," he mumbled, peering into the bucket of chicken.

This would probably be where an ordinary father would recount how he met his wife. But Rick Wolf never spoke about Rylie's mother. Ever. It was clearly too sore for him.

"Well, it *is* all," she said, chewing. "What, are you telling me you want grandkids? You clearly didn't even want *kids*."

"I'm not telling you nothin'," he said, shoving the bucket toward her. "Because since when have you ever listened to me anyway?"

True. He'd been so absent, mostly drunk, while she was growing up. And so Rylie had acted out. She'd gotten so used to being alone that when he was home and tried to tell her what to do, she fought back. They'd even had their share of fist fights, right in the living room of their house.

"Anyway," he said, leaning back and crossing his arms. "You gonna tell me why you're here?"

She froze with a drumstick halfway suspended between the plate and her mouth. "I told you. Visit."

"Right." He snorted, and for the first time, she almost saw a smile. But it wasn't a happy one. "You come all the way over here from Rapid City and you don't have a case? How many hours' drive is that? Eight?"

"Only six," she said, averting his eyes. They may have been estranged, but they were still related. And he had her number.

"Yeah. Right. You weren't anywhere near the neighborhood. So spill it. Why are you here?"

She sighed. "I was getting to that."

"Not fast enough," he remarked.

She stared at him, then shook her head, defeated. They would never come to a truce, would they? Finally, she dropped the chicken down on the plate, wiped her hands with a paper napkin, and pulled her phone out of her pocket. "Fine."

Rylie scrolled to the picture of Griffin Franklin and slid the phone over to him.

As he picked it up, she said, "Does that guy look familiar?"

13

Rick Wolf gave it a perfunctory glance. "Should he?"

"Look carefully," she prodded. "You might have seen him, twenty years ago."

"Nope," he said after another too-quick glance, shoving it over to her. "Never saw him before in my life."

She sucked in a breath. Why did he have to be so stubborn? "Dad, if you would just—"

"*No,*" he barked, cutting her off with a voice as severe as a punch to the gut.

She stared at him.

He blinked slowly, several times, clenching his hands in front of him. It looked as though he was trying to compose himself. Maybe it was something he'd learned at AA, because he never used to be one to hold his tongue. He'd been just as impulsive as she was. When he did speak, his voice was calmer.

He said, "I know what you are thinking. You are telling me this man might have something to do with what happened to us. Our family. And I'm telling you, right now, that I don't care."

Her mouth opened in her incredulity. "But Dad, how could you not—"

"Rylie. Let me finish," he said, his voice getting louder, sharper. "I have spent most of my life trying to get past what happened. They were, without a doubt, the darkest days of my life. And it is because I pulled myself out of that hole that I am still here today. I do not wish to jump back in. Do you understand?"

She nodded. Yes, deep down, she'd known that. She hadn't really wanted to open those old wounds in him, but she'd felt like there was no choice. Plus, she felt for sure that if there was new evidence, he'd come around.

But now, she realized it was a big mistake. "Yes. I guess."

They sat in silence for a long time. Rylie had lost her appetite. She gathered the food up and packaged it neatly. "I can save this for you? Leftovers."

He shook his head. "I don't want it," he mumbled, but to her, it was more like, *I don't want anything you can give me, so get out.*

She decided to leave it there, anyway. If nothing else, it would be a reminder that she was there. That she'd tried. Even if he thought she was just using him to get info on the case, she really did want to open the lines of communication again. She didn't know how else to prove it to him.

"All right," she said, finishing her soda and heading for the door. "Thanks, Dad. Be well."

He didn't respond.

She went outside and down the stairs to her car, staring at his red Ford Ranger. She peered inside it, wishing it would give her a glimpse into his life now, since he clearly wasn't going to. But though old, it was showroom clean. It didn't even have a dent in it.

She looked up at his apartment, hoping she'd see the blinds tented or moving slightly, any indication that he was watching her. That he cared.

But there was nothing.

Slowly, she slid into her own truck and thought about her drive out here. It was stupid to think he'd want to help. Where the tragedy had fed Rylie's curiosity and thirst for justice, it had simply stolen Rick's will to live. And he didn't want to revisit that. She couldn't blame him for not wanting to go back to the worst time of his life.

She was about to pull out when her phone rang. It was her partner, Michael. She wondered if he was as bored as she was. Probably not. Michael Brisbane was even keeled, and perfectly happy to have off days, with nothing to do but kick back and relax. He didn't need his adrenaline pumping all the time, like she did.

"Hey," she said as she lifted the phone to her ear.

"Wolf. Where are you?"

She imagined him, outside her apartment, knocking in vain. "In Wyoming. Visiting my dad."

"Ah. Well, get your butt on back here."

He sounded rushed, borderline excited. She wasn't silly enough to think it was because he missed her smiling face. So that meant one thing. "There's a case?"

"Yep," he said. "Right here in South Dakota. How quick can you get over here so we can check it out?"

She looked at the clock on her dash. It was noon. Though the trip here had been six hours, she knew she could do better than that. "I'll be there by four."

"Can you make it three?"

"What?"

15

"Kit said that if we don't get out there right away, she's going to assign it to another team."

"Fine," she said, and stomped on the gas as she headed for Interstate 86.

CHAPTER THREE

Rylie made it back into Rapid City in just under four and a half hours.

Of course, she'd gone ninety the whole way. If Michael had been with her, such a feat never would've been possible, because he would've been white knuckling it, the whole way, feet on the dashboard, asking her to slow down. The man preferred driving like an old lady.

She pulled into the apartment complex, a sprawling neighborhood of eight squat brick buildings, and drove to the back where his apartment was situated, pressed up against a field of tall yellow grass. The moment she knocked on the door, he answered, as if he'd been waiting by it for her. "Took you long enough."

"You wouldn't have liked how I was driving," she said, ignoring, as she always did, how movie-star handsome he was. He was effortlessly so, in his button-down shirt, open at the throat, and slacks, his typical uniform for the road. He forever had a dark smattering of stubble on his chin, even though he shaved constantly, and his dark hair was thick and wayward, framing gorgeous, ice-blue eyes.

"All right. So I assume that means I'm driving. Let me just get my keys." He pushed open the door to let her pass.

She stepped in. As much as she didn't like him behind the wheel, she was pretty exhausted from the ten hours of driving. Plus, he'd said it was right here in state. So maybe it would be a quick drive. "Probably a good idea. Where was the body . . ."

She trailed off as he said, "About two hours east of here. Pierre."

At this point, they'd known each other a few months, but she'd never actually been in his apartment before. Because it was at the back of the development, it was out of the way, and so he usually stopped at hers to pick her up before they went off on their cases. But as she looked around, her jaw dropped. "What happened here?"

The place looked like a magazine cover. It was all bright white walls and new fixtures, modern and effortlessly comfortable. She could see the general layout was the same as her place—kitchen and living area, combined, with a short hallway that led to the single bath and the bedroom, but that was where the similarities ended. The décor was sparse but refined, the only pop of color a green houseplant or a red accent pillow. It was no bachelor pad, that was for sure. That was, well, *her* place.

He scanned it, confused. "You like it?"

"Yeah . . . but how did you . .. when did you find the time to . . .?"

"Fixing up places is kind of a hobby of mine," he said. "I love those DIY shows on television. You know those twins? They really know their stuff.*"*

He whistled.

She stared at him. When she'd first met him, she was sure she had him pegged—he was a good-looking, egotistical playboy who used his looks and charm to get him places. But he'd proven to be nothing like that. Of course, he was good-looking, but he was self-deprecating, too. And while he clearly had an eye for pretty women, he became a bit of a bumbling mess around them. And as far as using his charm? He did that, too, but only when it was necessary to help them solve a case. She'd spent so much of her time with him over the months, and yet he was constantly saying things, even now, that surprised her. "How did I not know that?"

He shrugged and scratched the back of his neck, something he only did when he was embarrassed about something. It was kind of adorable. She really hated herself for thinking that, but it was true.

And that was just great. He must've thought she was a slob, with no female instinct for homemaking whatsoever. And he'd be right. Here she was, unsure about asking him for help as to the color of her walls and dreading hanging a certain picture, when she had the Mr. Fix-Everything as a partner. "You should've told me! I would've let you help with my place."

"I can still help. Just say the word." He came up close to her and smiled.

Too close for simple partners. She had to take a step back, even though she kind of liked it. "Oh, I will."

He noticed the movement and cleared his throat, then took a step back himself. "Uh. Yeah." He jingled the keys. "Ready?"

She spun to step out. "I guess. I haven't even been back to my place, though."

"Oh. You haven't? Er . . . You want to . . ."

She shook her head. "Forget it." After seeing this place, she didn't want to be reminded of how badly she'd failed with her own apartment. "Let's just go."

"But you might want to pack a bag. It's getting late and we'll probably have to overnight at least."

"Really? So it's a big case? What's it about?" She narrowed her eyes at him, wishing she'd been home to get the call from Kit. Kit had called her, but she'd put her phone on silent when visiting with her father, knowing that he would be annoyed if she kept checking her phone. Rick Wolf wasn't one for technology. Never had been.

"I'll tell you on the way." Michael checked his phone. "But we should get on the road, so you'd better get packed."

She pointed to her truck. "I have a bag all ready."

"Wow. Someone was chomping at the bit for a new case," he said as he pulled the door closed. "I know the feeling."

He might have, but there was no way he was excited as Rylie. He was steadier, rock-like, and not easily emotional. He'd always been very good at calming her excitability.

"You clearly weren't so excited that you couldn't do anything else, Mr. Fix-It," she said as they went to her truck and she pulled out a duffel. She threw it in the back of his, and seconds later, they were heading out of Rapid City on Interstate 86.

Interstate 86 was otherwise known as the Highway Thru Hell. That was one of many names for the infamous stretch of road that spanned several states, from Seattle, Washington, to Eau Claire, Wisconsin. It was aptly named, since terrible things had been known to happen on this road, everything from hitchhiker serial killings to kidnappings. It was pretty shocking, considering most of the towns along the route were remote, one stoplight outposts with a gas station and a single hotel that saw barely any overnight guests. The body count had been so shockingly high, and crime so prevalent, that it had demanded the FBI set up a new office in Rapid City, specifically, to deal with it.

And a few months ago, Rylie Wolf had gotten tapped for it.

Well, it wasn't so much that she'd gotten *tapped*. More like, *forced out*. She'd locked horns with her supervisor, Bill Matthews, one too many times. He was nothing like her—he was lazy, silly, and had been promoted to the job by sheer nepotism, so she'd never respected him. And unlike the other people in the office, like her friend Cooper Rich, she'd never been good at faking respect.

But as much as she'd hated the idea of coming back east, especially Wyoming, which held a lot of personal demons for her, the new post had been good for her. She'd expected to be bored, sent out to pasture like this. But there had proven to be a lot of work for her out here, a lot of juicy cold cases to sink her teeth into. She'd solved many of them, gotten accolades, and her star was rising.

Plus, though she'd never wanted a partner before, she had to admit, Michael Brisbane wasn't half bad.

Except, of course, as another car whizzed by him in the fast lane. And then another.

She checked the speedometer. As always, he was going exactly seventy miles per hour. The speed limit on this road was seventy-five, but he reserved that for passing.

Which he never did, because no one on the road went this slow.

She looked out the window at the yellow plains of South Dakota. It was flat and boring, with only the occasional tree now and then, and an overpass or stop with a farm or house. She yawned and said, "Okay, so this case? What's it about?"

"Yeah," he said, turning down the country music on the radio station. "Two women were murdered in their homes right along the highway. One in Pierre, one in Sweeten. They were living alone, and the killer somehow forced their way into the house in the middle of the night. No sign of burglary or anything like that. Kit thinks there might be some connection because of the way both of the women were killed."

"Which is?"

"They were all smothered. With a pillow. And the two murders happened a couple of days apart."

She frowned. Something about that tickled her mind. "Case files?"

"On their way. Kit said she'd have the PD send them to us as soon as she got her hands on them. You can check my phone."

She grabbed his phone from the cup holder and opened it. By now, she knew his password as well as her own. His phone was like his apartment—neat and orderly, without a blemish or fingerprint on the screen. She opened his email, but found no messages from Kit yet.

"Nothing yet." She scrolled down to check for messages again. Then again. And again. She sighed.

"Relax. She'll send it when she gets it."

Rylie sighed again. He said "relax" as if it were something easy for her to do. She never could relax. He should've known that by now.

"You ever think about . . . I don't know. Taking two?"

"What do you mean?"

"I mean, Wolf. Chill. Take a load off and let me get you there, first."

"No," she muttered. "The case is waiting for us to solve it. We need to—"

"What you need to do is unwind once in a while. It's not healthy to be go-go-go all the time."

Oh, now she understood. "Is this because I turned you down for dinner the other day? I told you, I had all that painting to do, and I wanted to get it done in case we got sent out on the road again. It wasn't—"

"No, it's not that."

Rylie got the feeling it definitely *was*. They went to dinner all the time, no problem. But the real reason she'd said no to this invite was because there'd been a strange tone to his voice when he'd asked her— he'd sounded overly charming and flirtatious, bordering on smarmy, like, *Hey baby, wanna go out*? And it had come completely out of the blue. They'd just been talking about the interviews they had to give, divvying them up, maybe flirting a little, but mostly trading good-natured jabs, when he switched gears and said they should go out. Have a few drinks. Maybe he hadn't meant it, but it had sounded like a date.

It had taken her by such surprise that she'd frozen up at once. Made excuses. Yes, she liked him. Quite a lot. Maybe even more than any man she'd ever met. But a date? When everything between them as partners had been going so well?

She wasn't sure she wanted to cross that bridge.

When she stared at him, confused, he said, "I just don't want you to burn yourself out. I know more than a couple people on the force whose life became the job. It doesn't end well."

She knew he was probably right.

But she couldn't help it. The tickling in her mind didn't go away. In fact, it got stronger. "Isn't there a case like that already? I could've sworn . . . two women who were strangled in South Dakota."

She reached into the back of the truck, where they'd kept a huge pile of cold cases from the past few years that had happened along the route. They were all in a banker's box, and out of her grasp, so she gave up. She'd have to look when they stopped.

She grunted and turned back, not expecting Michael to remember the case, since there were hundreds of cases in those boxes. But he nodded. "Yeah . . . now that you mention it, it does ring a bell. It was on one of the Indian Reservations, wasn't it?"

"Was it?" She glanced back at the files. She *really* wanted to know. It was itching at her, making her anxious.

He looked over at her, studying her. "How much coffee have you had?"

She drummed her hands on her thighs and checked his speedometer. He was going sixty-eight. "A lot." She didn't want him to stop, now. They had to keep going.

"I thought so." He started to pull slowly over to the side of the road.

"Wait. What are you doing?" she asked him, confused. She just wanted to get there.

He motioned to the back of the truck. "Get the files, first. We have a long way to go. And you need something to distract you. If you look at my speedometer one more time, heads are going to roll."

CHAPTER FOUR

Ten minutes after pulling over to the side of the road, Michael started his truck up again, and they proceeded along the route to the crime scene.

Now, thank goodness, Rylie had something to keep her occupied. She'd found the folder they'd both been thinking about. Otherwise, she could be a bear to deal with.

But he liked it. He was the only one, it seemed, who could calm her down. They were good together. He was good for her.

If only he could figure out a way to get her to realize that.

But for Rylie Wolf, it was all about business. Every time she showed up, her mind was squarely on whatever they were doing for the FBI. When he'd tried to get personal with her, to suggest they go out for drinks or dinner or whatever, she shot him down. She'd actually said that to him, the other day, when he'd asked her to go out for dinner and drinks: *What? Dinner? Why? It's not like we have a case.*

Until then, he'd thought they really liked each other. They got along great. They made each other better. But right then? He had his doubts. It was like she couldn't stand to be with him, if they weren't on the clock.

He looked over at her as she sat there, tapping her fingers on the armrest, nose buried in the case file. She couldn't see spending any time with him unless it was for their job. Yes, he understood it. They did spend *a lot* of time together for their job. But he knew there was another side of her than FBI agent. More and more, he wanted to see it.

But more and more, she seemed to want to hide it from him.

He got it. He'd fouled up. The one time she'd tried to let him into her past, the tragedy of what had happened to her mother and sister, he'd closed up. Because it'd been too similar to his own past, and he wasn't ready to revisit that anytime soon. Since then, he'd tried to be helpful. To work with her to find peace.

That wasn't what he wanted, though. He wanted to have fun. Go out dancing. Kick back with some beers and conversation. Have a date. Just a night where they weren't bogged down by all this heavy shit.

As he looked over at her, though, he couldn't picture Rylie ever being like that. It was like her past had completely swallowed up her ability to have any fun whatsoever. And no matter what he tried to do to start it, she always shut him down.

"Ah, now I remember this case," she mumbled, reading it. "You were right. It did happen on an Indian Reservation. But it's not really all that similar. The two women were strangled, not smothered. It could be related, though. The reservation's only fifty miles from Sweeten."

"Hmm," he muttered, still wondering what she'd look like with her hair down, letting loose on the dance floor. Smiling, her face flushed, beautiful.

He doubted he'd ever see such a thing.

Then he gritted his teeth. What the hell was he doing? Was he actually . . .*falling for his partner?*

Warning bells went off in his head. He tried to suppress the thoughts, but that only sent them screaming to the forefront of his mind. His mind trailed to what it would be like to kiss her lips. Would she smile at him, then? Maybe even forget this world of crime and mayhem and death they shared, just for a little while?

She said something about the case, but he missed it. Instead, he said, "Hmm."

Rylie clucked her tongue. "Are you even listening to me?"

"Yeah, sure," he mumbled, staring out the window so he wouldn't look at the lips he'd just imagined kissing.

"Then what was the last thing I said?"

"Something about . . . how the murders weren't . . ." He let out a laugh. "All right. Fine. What did you say?'

She rolled her eyes. "I said that both murders on the reservation happened at night, when the women were home alone. But over a year ago."

Hoping his face wasn't blushing, as it sometimes did when he thought of such things—he was like a twelve-year-old boy when it came to that--he motioned to his phone. "Kit send the case files yet?"

She opened his phone and stared at it. "Oooh. Yes," she said, as excited as a kid in a candy store.

This was what she lived for, after all. Maybe it was too much to think she had that fun-loving side. Maybe she'd been so damaged in her life, that wasn't possible.

No. He didn't believe that. He'd been through traumatic experiences, himself. And while it'd been buried for a time, while he'd once thought he'd never be able to smile again, eventually, he pulled himself out from under it. Maybe Rylie just needed someone to pull back the charred layers to get to the part of her that could still feel . . .

He was stirred from those thoughts when she snapped her fingers. "Hello?"

"Uh . . yeah?"

"Oh, my God. Why are you zoning? Are you okay?" she asked, staring at him curiously.

"Yeah. Just . . ." He blinked hard. "The road is tough. Same old thing. Putting me in a trance. You know?"

"Crack a window. You want me to drive?"

He powered the window down an inch so cool air hit his face. It helped. "No. I'm good. What were you saying?"

"I was just saying that the first victim in the new case, the one in Pierre, wasn't smothered in her home. She was killed at a motel off of 86. But the more recent victim, the one from Sweeten, was killed in her home. Right outside the back door. Looks like the intruder entered through there. She had an alarm system but she might not have known how to use it, because it was disarmed."

Michael listened as Rylie relayed the details, clinically, robotically. After being on the force for as long as they had been, it was easy to separate their business from the horrors of the cases they were looking into, to put the emotion of it aside and concentrate on getting the work done. But rarely had he seen Rylie show any emotion at all. When it came to her job, she was always on. "Then what's your thought. You think these two cases are related?"

"To each other?" She nodded. "Definitely. Similar MO, similar victims, young women who were alone, over the past few days. But to the murders on the reservation? Not sure. They happened over a year ago, and they were strangled. Victims didn't know each other. A couple of male suspects were interviewed and released, not enough evidence to convict. Likely, no. We shouldn't rule it out, though."

"Okay, so where are we headed?"

"Sweeten. It's closer, and the scene of the most recent murder."

He gave her a thumbs-up and pushed on the gas, pushing slightly over seventy. Rylie would be happy about that.

Of course, not happy enough. He felt like everything he did wasn't enough for her. After all, though he hated not pulling his weight, and he tried to keep up with her . . . he always felt like she was competing. Like she wanted to best him. The thing was, she usually did. She was fearless. Full of determination. Sometimes she acted rash and insane, but it was a good thing. Sometimes he was over-cautious. If it hadn't been for Rylie, they wouldn't have such a stellar record. She was effective, that was for sure.

Almost too effective. Sometimes, he felt like he always had to be on, too. Like he could never take a breath, go out, relax, have a good time. And whenever he suggested it to her, she usually made him regret it and feel like a slacker.

But damn, how he wanted it.

His mind trailed to the thought of her, on a dance floor. Doing something just because it felt good. No, it seemed like she was intent on punishing herself because her sister's kidnapper had never been found. Like she couldn't rest and let her hair down, as long as the mystery was still out there.

He tried to imagine her just walking casually down a street, or in a park, maybe holding his hand. It just seemed so incongruous. Not Rylie. She never turned off.

Maybe she never would. All they had was a necklace, and a fingerprint on a mirror that belonged to a person who might or might not have crossed paths with her sister, years ago. It was practically nothing. After twenty years, the chances of learning anything about Maren Wolf were slim.

"The victims are similar," she was saying, scrolling through the file on the phone. "But they could just be crimes of opportunity."

Opportunity, he thought to himself. *Yeah. If I wait until she finds out what happened to her sister, nothing will happen. I am never going to get the opportunity to tell her how I feel.*

She clapped her hands sharply, and he realized he'd taken his foot off the gas, dropping their roll to under sixty.

"Come on! Move it! There are crimes that need solving!" she shouted at him, like a drill sergeant.

He did as he was told, just as a sign that said SWEETEN 12 appeared in the distance. That's where they were headed. Yes, there were crimes that needed solving. And as long as they were out there, everything else, he guessed, would just have to wait.

26

CHAPTER FIVE

Rylie had finished perusing the file as they finally pulled off the exit at Sweeten, shortly after five. Sweeten was another one-horse town with a gas station and a hotel. There was a small supermarket, a few blocks away from the Interstate, and a tiny development of fifties ranch houses behind it. Other than that, the place was surrounded by farmland.

The GPS led them to a loop of fifties ranch houses, so close to the Interstate that they could see the ramp they'd just pulled off of as they turned onto the street. It wasn't hard to find the house—there was police tape around it, and a couple of patrol cars parked in the driveway. The home itself was modest, half-brick, with peeling pink paint. The lawn could've used a good mowing, and there was a flowerbed near the front walk that needed weeding, but other than that, it seemed to be well-kept.

As Rylie stepped out, she greeted the officer who was standing outside, flashing her credentials. "Hi," she said, "I'm Agent Wolf from the FBI, and this is Michael Brisbane, my partner. Were you the first on the scene?"

The man was more of a boy, so tall he looked like a basketball player, making Michael look small, and Michael was over six feet. He was hunched as if he was embarrassed about his height, and he had reddish hair and freckles. "Yeah, I was," he said, his voice cracking. "They called in the FBI on this? I didn't know that."

Brisbane nodded. "There's a possibility this murder might be related to one that happened up north in Pierre. Do you know of that one?"

He shook his head. "I'm just—we haven't had no murders around here ever. This one . . ." He hung his head. "It was terrible. Awful. I didn't sleep at all last night."

Of course, Michael was sympathetic, giving the guy a pat on the shoulder. "What's your name, buddy?"

He looked down for his name tag, but must've forgotten to put it on. "Geez. I'm Matt. Matt Walker."

"You been on the force long?"

He shook his head. "This is my first year. My dad's chief."

"Gotcha," Michael went on, smiling at the kid. Michael could always put people at ease. That was his specialty. She was more of the shark, the person who got answers. They worked well together that way—he softened people, so she could move in for the kill and get what they needed.

"Mind if we go in and look around?" Rylie asked, not waiting for an answer as she pulled open the front door and stepped in. There was a clean hallway with a tiled floor, old, flowered wallpaper, and a rather new-looking security system panel right beside the door.

She stared at it. "So this wasn't engaged last night, huh?"

The boy looked up and seemed surprised to see her, standing there. He'd been busy pouring out his sorrows to Michael. He said, "Oh, no. It wasn't. It had been, according to the security company. But then the victim—uh, her name was Marie Bottoms—she turned it off."

"She did? Why?"

"Neighbor next door said she'd recently split from her husband. She thought that the victim didn't know how to use it."

"Her husband?"

Officer Walker nodded. "Yeah. Lance Bottoms. Lives up in Pierre, as of a few weeks ago. I think he's shacking up with his secretary, from the rumors. We haven't been able to get in touch with him. Left messages, though."

Rylie looked around. The place smelled like canned rose air freshener, and was neat, with rather inexpensive, particle-board furnishings. All indicative of new homeowners who'd just recently set up house together. "She was mid-twenties, right?"

"Twenty-six," he said. "She grew up around here. My parents knew her parents. We're all pretty close in this community. Can't believe anyone would do this."

Now it made sense why he was so torn up. She motioned down the hallway. "Where was the body found?"

He pointed down the hallway, toward the kitchen. She went through the dark, modest kitchen with the oak cabinets and white laminate counters, and saw the open back door right away. When she pointed to it, he nodded. "No sign of forced entry, correct?"

"Yeah. Either the door was open, or she let the person in. She was laying out on this step, halfway in the kitchen, halfway in the living room, right inside the door. Facing up, her pajamas on. The pillow was still over her face." He shook his head and covered his eyes with his hand, as if to shield his tears from them. "Worst thing I ever saw."

Rylie had seen the pillow before, in the photos attached to the file— it had zig-zag stripes on it. Now, she noticed the sofa, right next to the door, had the same pattern. "The killer used the victim's pillow," she murmured.

Officer Walker nodded. "That's right."

The living area had a big, slightly stained couch, a television on a flimsy table, a massive ottoman, scattered with what looked like strings and beads. But the biggest piece of furniture in the place was a giant plastic shelving system with almost a hundred drawers. Rylie opened one of the drawers and looked inside. She found more beads. So Marie was a crafter. She'd heard that craft supplies were a bit of an obsession—this was her proof. "She liked to make things, huh?"

The officer shrugged. "I guess."

Rylie crouched in front of the area where the body had lain, imagining it set out as she'd seen in the photographs attached to the file. Something like this was the last thing this woman had seen. She could see the whole scene—Marie checking the back door to make sure it was closed before heading off to bed, only to have this killer meeting her there, grabbing the pillow from the couch, holding it tight over the woman's body as she struggled against him.

"Do you know who called it in? Was it the alarm company?" Michael asked, pacing around the kitchen and looking out into the backyard.

"No, it was the neighbor. She said she felt bad for Marie. Her husband had just left her, and so Marie wasn't in a good spot. Took a trip to visit family out in Wisconsin last week, after the news, but came back, was pretty lonely. So the neighbor stopped by in the morning to see if she needed anything—I guess they sometimes had coffee together— and found her like that."

"Neighbor?" Michael pointed to the right and the left.

"Over there," Officer Walker said, pointing to the green house next door.

"What's her name? We'll have to talk with her," Rylie said. "Did she say she heard or saw any signs of a disturbance?"

"Abby. Abby Foster. Nope. Nothing."

29

"And you asked around with the other neighbors?" Rylie asked, still checking around for anything they might have missed. She lowered her head so her ear was against the ground, searching for any evidence under the couch. But it was clean.

"Yeah, well, the guy across the street works night. And the couple on the other side were on vacation. So it's only this woman, Abby."

Rylie nodded and looked around, spotting on the entertainment center a framed wedding photograph. The man and woman in wedding attire were standing in profile, staring at each other, deep in love. Rylie could see traces of that woman—her bright red hair, her pale skin— from the photos she'd gotten of the crime scene, but that was where the similarities ended. In such a short period of time, her life had fallen apart.

That's the way things happen, Rylie thought. *One day, everything is just perfect and the next, it can all slip away.*

She studied the man's profile. He was a head taller than her, lean, and handsome, with a thick moustache and a bit of a receding hairline. She wondered what had led him to stray. Was it the secretary? Or was there more?

In cases like this, the first suspect was always the spouse. It was even more suspicious that they hadn't been able to get in touch with him.

Rylie nodded, signaling she was done, and stepped out into the backyard. Michael thanked the officer and followed. When they went out to the stone patio, she looked around. There was a privacy fence there, at least six feet high, as well as abundant landscaping. Even if any of the neighbors had been looking out last night, it would have been difficult to see anything.

"What are you thinking?" Michael asked as she went to the gate at the side of the house. They'd already dusted for fingerprints—she'd seen it in the report and could see remnants of it on the latch. Nothing. So she opened it and went through.

"Probably someone who knew she'd be home alone."

"You thinking a crime of passion by the husband?"

"Could be. But probably not if the Pierre murder is related. We'll have to see." Rylie pointed to the green house next door. "Think we should talk to the Foster woman."

He nodded. "It's interesting that he didn't have a murder weapon on him. That he used whatever he could find at the crime scene."

30

"Yeah. Which makes me wonder if those murders on the reservation are related—just a killer using whatever he could find at the moment."

She knocked on the door. A young woman with short, dark orange hair and tattoo sleeves on her arms opened it a moment later. "Yes?"

Michael showed his credentials. "Hello, Mrs. Foster, I'm Michael Brisbane from the FBI, and this is my partner, Rylie Wolf. We'd like to ask you some questions about your neighbor Marie's murder?"

She nodded and ushered them in. "Of course, of course! I've been frantic since it happened. We don't get things like this ever. It's so safe here, or at least, I thought." She shivered as she led them to the living room. It was a sunken area with threadbare carpet and paneled walls, and old, mismatched furniture. "Can I get you guys anything to drink?"

Rylie shook her head and sat on a flowered sofa. "So you discovered the body this morning?"

She nodded. "Most terrible thing! That poor woman. We were friends, you know. I'd just moved here from California because I got a job in the capital. And I'd only been here a day or so when she knocked on the door and introduced herself. Brought over cookies."

Michael smiled.

Abby Foster took her phone from the pocket of her jeans and held it up. There was a silver, beaded loop hanging from one side of it. "See this? She made this for me. She was very talented."

Rylie squinted. "What is it?"

"A cell phone charm! Cute, huh? So different. She had a great business. She was always sending out packages to people, making free ones for the people she knew. Said it was good advertising. She was very sweet." Her eyes turned stormy. "That husband of hers was *not*, though."

"No?"

"Oh, no. You'd say hi to him and he'd look the other way! He was a real jerk. I knew they were having problems. I got the feeling he was really controlling. He didn't like me coming over there, so I used to come over for coffee after he left. Then a couple weeks ago, she told me he'd left her for his secretary!" She shook her head. "Total jerk. She was beside herself. Didn't know what to do. So she went out of state to visit her family. When she came back a couple days ago, she seemed better. She told me she was going to get the backbone to hire a good divorce lawyer and fight him for all his money."

31

Michael raised an eyebrow. "So you think the two of them were at odds?"

"I know it," she said, sitting on the recliner across from them and slapping her thighs. "She was more reserved, quieter. It was that husband of hers that was the troublemaker."

"So you think that Lance Bottoms could have—"

"*Definitely*," she said with a nod. "I knew it from the moment I met him. He's shifty as hell. Didn't surprise me in the least he had a girlfriend on the side. Probably more than one. The women went all crazy for him. I even saw one of them, dropping him off at his house late at night. That was a couple months ago, when I first moved in. I didn't tell Marie, but . . . poor girl. He was playing her. And now he's gone and killed her."

Rylie looked at Michael, who said, "You didn't see anyone lurking around her house last night, though?"

She shook her head. "I had a good book, and a bubble bath calling my name. I fell asleep. Woke up after one. Never saw or heard a thing. Wish I had." She sighed. "Not very neighborly of me. Last time I saw her, it was in passing, yesterday. I was out getting my mail and saw she was home from her parents' place in Wisconsin. That's when she told me she was getting a lawyer. I told her, good for her, and we made plans to have a coffee chat at her place this morning."

"Does she usually set the alarm, do you know?"

Abby laughed. "Actually, she didn't. The thing annoyed her. Lance handled all of that for her. But she never seemed to get it to work right. She tried to get me to help her, but I don't know anything about alarms. I think Lance knew that she was having trouble with it. Maybe he wanted it that way. And so . . ."

Rylie made a mental note of that. It made sense that her husband could've exploited her lack of knowledge about the alarm, shown up to the back door, and surprised her. Maybe he'd only shown up to talk, but then he'd lost control. There were so many possibilities, but the end result was the same—Lance Bottoms was definitely their number one person of interest in this crime.

Rylie stood up. "Well, thank you," she said, as Michael Brisbane rummaged through his pocket and pulled out a business card.

He handed it to Abby. "Call us if there's anything you need or want to discuss."

"Sure will," she said, leading them out to the front door. When they got there, she looked out and gasped. "Speak of the devil!"

Rylie craned her neck to see what had captured the young woman's attention. There was a red sportscar parked behind the police car, and a man in a suit, with dark sunglasses, was climbing out. "Is that—"

"Yep. That's him. That's Lance Bottoms, the jerk," she snarled, scowling at him. "If you really want to get to the bottom of this, you'd bring him in and make him tell you what happened."

"Thanks," Rylie said, rushing down the path to intercept him, Michael Brisbane at her heels.

CHAPTER SIX

Rylie rushed across the Bottoms' property, meeting up with the man as he stalked across the unmanicured lawn. He looked harried, almost angry, a stark difference from the photograph, where he'd been smiling lovingly down at his new wife. His hair had receded a lot more, leaving a full bald spot at the top, but he was still fit and handsome, dressed in a formal, tailored three-piece suit that made him stand out.

Before she could say a word, he wailed, "Get out of my way! Oh, Marie! My poor Marie," and shoved her out of the way.

Michael intervened, then, grabbing the man by the shoulders. "Hold on, there. Hold on," he said, speaking in a firm but calm voice. "It's a crime scene. You can't—"

"It's my *home!*" he sobbed, trying to shake himself free. "And that is my *wife!*"

Michael held firm. "Slow down. We know all that. Lance Bottoms, I presume?"

The man stopped struggling and looked at the two of them in confusion. "Yeah. Who the hell are you?"

"FBI," Michael said. "We're investigating your wife's murder."

At the word "murder", the man's face crumpled and reddened. "What . . . what happened? Someone came in and . . . ?"

Rylie nodded. "She was smothered by a pillow at the back door of the house last night."

"Last night?" He closed his eyes and let out a long, mournful wail, then fell to the grass on his knees, burying his face in his hands. "Not my Marie! Who would do such a thing?"

Rylie looked over at Abby's house. Abby was watching the whole thing from the picture window in her house, and seemed unmoved. Indeed, it was quite a performance. In Rylie's experience, murdering husbands always did overdo it when it came to grief. This little act only made her more suspicious. "Can we ask you where you were last night, Mr. Bottoms?"

He blinked and looked at her, and when he did, she noticed there were no tears. "I was . . . in the city. At a friend's. That's where I work, so sometimes I stay there overnight when I can't get back."

Michael said, "Can we get the name and address of that friend of yours so we can confirm?"

The man pressed his lips together. "What? Why? You can't possibly think that I did something like this? I hope that's not what you're insinuate—"

"It's purely procedural," she murmured as he stood up and wiped the grass from his knees. "I was told the police tried to get in touch with you?"

"Yes . . ." he said cautiously, guardedly. "I suppose they did. My phone died, and I couldn't get a charge until I was in my car on the way over here. I was kind of . . . preoccupied. Someone at work told me about it. They saw it on the news. When I heard, I came right over."

"Is that right? What had you so preoccupied?" Michael asked.

He frowned. "Why are you asking. I should . . . I should get a lawyer, I think."

"We just want to know so we can help find your wife's killer," Rylie snapped, getting annoyed. For someone so distraught over his wife's death, he certainly seemed defensive of his own hide. "Your neighbor said you left your wife, and that you were seeking a divorce?"

He took a step back, clearly offended that she already knew so much about him. His eyes drifted to the neighbor's house. "Yes, we have been going through a rough patch, but . . . what else did she say about me?"

"When was the last time you spoke to your wife?" Michael asked.

"I don't know . . ." he shrugged. "She went out to visit her family in Wisconsin. She called and left me a message. I'm a busy man. I didn't even know she'd gotten back."

"You didn't? So you haven't discussed the divorce at all?"

He shook his head. "No. My lawyer's in the process of putting the paperwork together. She wasn't happy about it. But like I told her, I couldn't stay. Carrie—that's my girlfriend—she lives in Pierre. I've been staying with her. I haven't been back here in weeks."

He seemed sincere, now. Anything, though, to cover his own backside. Rylie paused to look at Michael and said, "She was having issues with the alarm. It's thought that because she didn't know how to work it, the killer might have gained entrance. Did you not show her how to use it?"

His eyes narrowed. "I showed her. Again and again. She couldn't get the hang of it. Marie . . . she was more of a creative type. She made crafts and stuff. Sold them online. She wasn't technical, like me. And she was absent-minded. I wouldn't put it past her to have forgotten it altogether." He dragged his hands down his face. "I feel responsible."

"So you didn't know that Marie had come back from Wisconsin and was securing her own lawyer?" Rylie said.

His brow wrinkled. "I don't know why she—I told her that we could use my own attorney and we'd be able to settle this easily." He pressed his lips together and let out a growl. "Wait. Who was she talking to? That meddling neighbor Abby? Is that what got this idea in her head?"

Before Rylie could say anything, he stomped past her, toward Abby's house. Abby had disappeared from the window, but there was murder in Lance's eyes. He might have launched himself onto her property if it hadn't been for Michael, holding him back.

"Wait, big guy," Michael said calmly. "She didn't say anything. We're just trying to—"

"Right, she didn't say anything? Some friend she was to Marie. Bet you she didn't tell you that whenever Marie was away, she'd come by the house in her short shorts and tight top and come on to me. All the time." He scoffed. "She's a real piece of work, that one."

Michael held up his hands. "Okay, okay. We're not accusing you of anything. And Abby simply said that when your wife came back, she'd be getting a new lawyer. That's all. So if you can tell us where you were, last night, we can let you go."

He let out a big sigh and seemed to calm down slightly. "All right. Fine. I was with Carrie. We worked late—she's my secretary. We were in the office until ten. Security could vouch for that. And then we drove to Lido's—that's an Italian restaurant near the capital, and we had a late dinner. Then we went back to her apartment. There are security cameras there, too."

Michael marked this all down, and Rylie's lips twisted. All of that was easily verifiable. It was likely a good hour drive to Pierre from here. Time of death was around midnight. That meant that their best suspect had a pretty solid alibi.

Meaning that he was probably in the clear, and they needed to look elsewhere. "Thank you, Mr. Bottoms."

He turned to the door. "Can I . . . go inside?"

Rylie went to the door and called for Officer Walker. "You'll have to stay with the officer since it's an active crime scene," she told him.

He took a deep breath and followed the officer inside.

When they were alone on the front stoop, Rylie looked at Michael. "I wonder if she picked up some stalker on her trip, who followed her home?"

"Possibly."

"Unless," she said, deep in thought. "It was just random. But then how would they know she was alone, unless she'd gone advertising it to people? Maybe it was someone who knew Lance, and that Lance wasn't living there? That would make sense to tie it to the Pierre motel murder, right?"

Michael nodded. "And I don't know about those strangling cases. They were a year ago. Seems odd that he'd wait that long, then strike twice in two days."

She slid into the passenger's seat of the car, her nose already buried back in the case file. "I guess we should go on to the next crime scene. On to Pierre."

"Aye-aye, Captain," Michael said, mock-saluting her, starting the truck, and pointing it in the direction of I-86 Eastbound. "On to Pierre."

CHAPTER SEVEN

"Shit."

Rylie looked up from the case files, momentarily confused. She expected to see a deer rushing across the street or something. It was a rare moment when Michael Brisbane uttered an expletive. He was far too calm for that.

But there was nothing. The road was clear. They were coming into a little more traffic, but that was because they were getting close to the capital. Other than that, everything seemed fine, except that her partner was now fishing in his pockets and the cup holders for something. Not finding what he was looking for, he opened up the armrest console between them and dug his hand in there.

"Problem?"

"Yeah. You have a dollar?"

"Yes . . . For what?" She reached into her purse and pulled it out. It seemed like an awfully inconvenient time to stop for coffee, especially since they'd wanted to get to Pierre before sundown.

He glanced over at her, noting the files on her lap. "Ah. You were too busy with your nose in the files to see that giant yellow sign we passed."

"What did it . . ." she began, but then they came upon another one. STOP AND PAY TOLL $1 ONE MILE AHEAD. "Oh."

"Yeah," he said, taking the dollar from her. "Oh."

"I thought that there was a moose in the road, judging from how you reacted."

"What do you mean?"

"You say *I'm* uptight. Hey. Since when did they put tolls on I-86?" she asked in confusion. "I thought the road was toll-free until Minneapolis."

"Apparently not," he mumbled as he slowed for brake-lights up ahead. "Actually, I think I remember reading about it. They put it in last year. First toll booth in all of South Dakota."

"Bummer."

"Ah. You know how all these places are. All for a good cause. Using the revenue to repair the roads." He drummed his fingers on the steering wheel. "And I didn't say you were uptight. I said you could stand to relax and let loose a little. Not be always on the job, all the time."

"I'm not."

"You *are*."

"Well, I'm sorry," she said defensively. "Am I exhausting you, Bris?"

He paused for a moment and said, "No. But it can't be good for you. You should—I don't know. Just kick back with a few drinks and have a good time. Once. That's all."

She couldn't help but feel defensive. He thought she was a stick in the mud, her mind always on the job. And maybe in his eyes, she was—but that was because they were partners. She knew how to have a good time. For example . . .

Actually, as she thought about it, she realized she hadn't kicked back and relaxed *at all,* since coming to the area.

No wonder he thought she was lame. She'd forgotten how to relax.

Before she could say anything in response, he pulled through the toll lane and stopped for the collector, whose hand was already outstretched, waiting for the money. Michael casually powered down the window. "Hey there, nice day?" he said to the man.

Rylie almost laughed. Michael Brisbane could—and often did—carry on conversations with walls. This guy simply took his dollar and grunted.

Not that it deterred her partner in the least. He smiled as he powered up his window. "Have a good day."

Sometimes, she couldn't understand how he could be so cheerful. They were investigating the worst kind of crimes out there. Not to mention that she'd been stoic and quiet during most of their rides together, and yet he never let it get to him. He chattered on and on, stream of consciousness, no matter what. She'd never seen him have a bad day, a day when he wasn't smiling from ear to ear like some kind of circus clown.

If anyone could get her to chill out, it was probably him. And yet, when he'd asked her out, she'd turned him down. But it wouldn't be so bad to relax for one night. In fact, it would probably be good for her.

"How about this?" she said, clapping her hands in front of her. "When we stop for dinner tonight, I'll have a couple beers, and I won't talk about the case at all. Okay?"

He didn't say anything.

"Okay?" she repeated.

He snorted. "I'll believe it when I see it."

She wrinkled her nose at him. Did he really think she was that dull? Well, she'd show him.

Shortly after the toll booth, the signs for Pierre came into view. "This is the exit," she told him, pointing.

He navigated to the right lane and took the ramp. Sure enough, the sign for the Easy Rest Hotel was visible from the off-ramp, already glowing, even though the sun hadn't yet set.

Good thing they'd brought their bags. There was still a lot of investigative work to be done. She wasn't sure how she felt about staying in a place where a woman had been murdered, though. She was about to look to see if there were any other hotels nearby, when he said, "Hey, they have a steakhouse!"

She groaned. The man's appetite was just about as unyielding as his smile.

"Think your stomach can wait long enough for us to check out the crime scene?" she asked him as he pulled to the stop sign at the end of the ramp.

"Putting off your promise to me, huh? I thought so."

She mimicked his voice for a little bit, then sighed. Okay, so, he was right. But she really did want to see this crime scene. "Make a right, here," she said. "Then the next left."

"Got it," he said, doing as she instructed. "So who is our victim for this crime?"

"Her name is Jessica Vega, twenty-three. From Minneapolis. She's a—oh. She was a dancer, at a club over there."

"Dancer, huh?"

The profession was important. It wouldn't have mattered, except that women in that line of work tended to have their share of admirers. Sometimes the most ardent admirers went too far and became stalkers.

But if that was the case, then this murder likely wasn't related to Marie Bottoms. And yet, the police reports for both murders showed virtually identical injuries. Both were overpowered and smothered by a pillow from the crime scene. It was too big of a coincidence to ignore.

They pulled up the long paved driveway, winding its way to the motel. It was a shame the motel had been the scene of a murder—it was actually pretty nice. Standing on a hill, the main office looked like an old farmhouse. But behind it were several guest houses, arranged in a crescent, with red doors. It was quaint and rustic, and well cared-for.

Michael tilted his head. "Does that house give you horror movie vibes? *Motel Easy Rest in Peace.*"

It hadn't, up until the moment he said it. Now, that was all she could think of. "You're right, I guess?"

Yet another reason to find another hotel.

They climbed up to the front porch and Brisbane reached forward, opening the door for her. "I keep expecting a guy to show up in a dress, with a butcher's knife," he said under his breath.

She frowned at him. "So that's why you're making me go first?"

His smile widened.

"Baby," she teased, marching inside. Inside, she found a normal reception office with a giant front desk and a large brochure rack of local attractions.

The young woman behind the desk had two thin, little-girl braids, despite looking about mid-twenties. She looked up from a Sudoku book as the bell rang over the front door. "Welcome to Easy Rest," she said pleasantly. "A room for the night?"

"FBI," Rylie said. "We're investigating the murder that happened here the night before last?"

She'd been reaching for a key off of the peg behind her, but she dropped her hand and sighed. "Oh, yeah."

Rylie noticed all of the other pegs had keys on them, too. "Hasn't been good for business, I'm sure."

The girl nodded and pointed to the open guest book in front of her. "Not at all. My parents are in Europe celebrating their twenty-fifth. I can't get in touch with them. But they are not going to be happy about this."

Rylie read the last name on the guest roster. *Jessie Vega,* written in loopy script. It was the same name she remembered from the police report.

"I'm Fiona Manning. Easy Rest is my family's pride and joy. My great-great-grandfather started it." The woman reached over and grabbed a different key and stood up. "Come on. I'll show you where it happened."

The girl led them through the rest of the building, past some rooms decorated with antique furnishings that did look a little bit like they'd come from a classic horror movie. Rylie could sense Michael eyeing it all suspiciously as they went through a kitchen with an old wood stove and out the back door.

"I'm guessing you don't have security cameras out here," Rylie remarked, scanning for them as they crunched over the gravel of the lot.

"That's right. My parents have been talking about getting them. But they haven't yet."

The girl led them to the last guest house in the semi-circle. It was getting dark now, and there were no streetlights to illuminate the parking lot. The only light seemed to come from the back porch of the house, which was quite a distance away. Remote and dark, it would've been dangerous for a woman, traveling alone, to be back here.

When she stopped in front to open it, Rylie noticed the police tape around the door. Michael said, "Door wasn't forced open?"

"Nope. But these doors aren't auto-lock like in most hotels, you know? They don't lock unless you lock them from the inside. And of course, there are chains, but you have to do that from inside." The girl pushed it open and demonstrated. "It's possible she didn't realize it wasn't locked. Anyway, I found her. Right here in the doorway, she was blocking it when I tried to push open the door. I usually do the cleaning. And I knocked and knocked. She didn't answer. "It's a little messy. They told me not to clean anything just yet."

The smell was musty, but when she flipped on the light, the inside looked spartan, but clean.

"Did you check her in that evening?" Michael asked.

She nodded. "I did. I'm doing it all! She was so nice. Really pretty. She was a little rattled, but we got to talking and I thought she was a nice woman."

It occurred to Rylie that if the killer wanted to commit a crime of opportunity, he could've easily gone after Fiona, alone in that office. "And it was just the two of you around here last night? No other guests?"

Fiona nodded. "Just the two of us," she said, and shuddered. "I guess I'm lucky."

Very lucky, Rylie thought. After all, the office door was open all night. The motel room would've been locked. So the killer wasn't just going after any random woman. "And you didn't see anyone at all?"

"No one." She looked around the room sadly. The bed wasn't made, and there was an open soda can on the dresser, but other than that, there wasn't much. "She came in pretty late that night, though."

"Did she say where she was heading?" Rylie asked.

Fiona nodded. "She wasn't from here. She was lost, that was the problem. From Minneapolis. She said she was heading west. Vegas, I think? I think she got confused because she said she'd wanted to stop and get a hotel room in the city, but then she drove on and realized there weren't many hotels for a long way. So she came back and got a room here. By then it was after one. She was really tired."

"Did she say what her purpose was? What she was planning to do?"

Fiona nodded. "She was visiting a boyfriend, I think? He thought he could get her a job out there? But she said that right then, she wanted to get a warm shower and get some good sleep, because she needed to get on the road bright and early." The woman threw up her hands. "That's why I got concerned when it got to be late morning and she still hadn't dropped off her key. So I went to check, and that's when I found her. Someone had taken one of her pillows and smothered her with it, I guess. It was covering her face."

"And there was nothing unusual at all that you might have heard, or seen?" Rylie asked, grasping at straws now.

"No. That's what's so crazy! I didn't see any other cars come up the drive. Like, I knew you were coming up because I saw your headlights. They flash in my eyes as you're coming up the driveway. I didn't see any, all night. And I was awake the whole time. Right there behind the desk."

Michael Brisbane walked into the room and looked around, then shrugged. "Anything else?" he asked Rylie.

Rylie shook her head and stepped outside. It was even darker, now, and definitely looked like a bad place to spend the night. But then again, it was on the outskirts of the city, remote and peaceful. People in the homes around here probably slept with their windows and doors open, and never thought twice about it.

"Thanks for your time," Michael said to the woman as they walked to the main office. As they did, Rylie stayed behind, looking around, trying to imagine just what had happened that night. Would the killer have come up the hill on foot? Or had he dimmed the headlights? Maybe he'd come from behind the guest houses. It looked as though there were buildings back there.

When they stopped at the side of the farmhouse office, Rylie was still looking all over, trying to recreate the crime in her mind. By now, Michael was used to her lingering, getting into the crime scene, so he didn't question it.

"What's back there?" she asked, pointing beyond the dumpsters, past a line of bushes to another building.

"Oh, them? Those are condos," she said.

"So it's possible the killer could've parked over there and come in from the back, and you never would've seen them. Right?"

The woman nodded. "Yeah, I guess. There's no fence there, so . . . yeah. If they came in through the bushes."

So that meant that really, anyone could've done it. But most likely, it was someone who was familiar with the area and the hotel, and was deliberately trying to avoid being noticed.

They said goodbye to Fiona, and Michael gave her a card, as usual. As they were leaving, Michael said, "So what have we got? Looks like we can't rule out that these two murders were committed by the same person."

"No, we cannot," she agreed. "I think we need to look into those murders on the reservation to see if we can tie them to this, or rule them out."

"Good plan. So . . . dinner?" He smirked at her.

She knew what that smirk meant. She hadn't eaten since breakfast, so she was hungry. But she also remembered her promise to him—no talking about the case during dinner. What she wanted most right now was to dig back into those files and try to find that connection.

But she guessed that would have to wait, at least for an hour or so, so she could show Michael Brisbane she wasn't all about the job.

"Fine," she said, managing a smile, wondering how quickly they could eat and be done so she could go back to looking for clues. "Dinner."

CHAPTER EIGHT

Wimpy's Steakhouse was a typical western saloon, with a long bar, wide-plank flooring and western décor like saddles, lassos, and artwork of bucking broncos on the walls. Peanut shells crunched under their feet as the hostess led them to a corner booth.

As she slid into the bench seat, Michael said, "So . . . shots?"

She looked up from the drink menu. "I said I'd have a couple drinks. You don't want to have to carry me out of here."

He shrugged. "Just thought it would help loosen you up."

The waitress came by for the drink order, and she said, "I'll have a margarita on ice, salt the rim."

He gave her a pouty face—he was the only fully-grown man who could pull that off without looking ridiculous—and said, "All right. Give me a Pine Stout."

When the waitress left, he leaned in. "So, tell me what's new with you."

She laughed. They'd spent enough time together over the months that everything she wanted to tell him, she already had. He knew her better than most people. "Nothing's new. Except for the case. But I'm not allowed to talk about that. Remember?"

He pointed to her thumb. She'd taken the bandage off last night, but it was still swollen. "What happened there?"

"I smashed it with a hammer," she admitted.

"Yeah?" His lips twisted in amusement.

"Yes, apparently, those DIY shows are not going to be banging down my door, anytime soon, wanting me to do an episode." He laughed, and opened his mouth to ask her more, but before he could, she said, "So how did you get so good at home improvement? Just watching television?"

He shrugged. "When I was young, we were pretty poor. I had to work summers. I worked for a design firm, helping rich people fix up their homes."

"Oh . . . this was in . . . Haven?"

He nodded slowly. He'd told her the name of the town in North Dakota where he'd spent his childhood years. Haven. She'd never be able to forget that, because of the way he'd spoken about it. There'd been pain in his eyes. Hurt. *I'm not ever going back to my hometown in North Dakota. I can't.* When she'd asked him why, he'd only told her, *Maybe I'll tell you sometime.*

If she was ever going to find out what had happened to him in Haven, this seemed like the best time. It was probably the only thing she wanted to know more than who had smothered those girls. "So . . ."

Just as she was about to broach the subject, the waitress arrived, tossing down cardboard coasters and putting their drinks down. "Can I take your order?"

Rylie hadn't looked over the menu. She glanced at the first thing. "I'll have the petite ribeye with baked potato and butter, and the vegetables."

The waitress wrote it down and looked at Michael. "Give me the biggest steak you've got."

She raised an eyebrow. "That's 48 ounces, are you--"

His eyes went wide. "Uh, no." He scanned the menu. "The porterhouse is good. Thanks."

The waitress took their menus and headed off, and he took a sip of his porter. "So . . ."

Was he trying to change the subject on her? She quickly said, "So you were telling me all about your childhood in Haven."

The smile fell from his face. "I don't think I was talking about that."

She smiled. "Yeah, you were."

This time, he took a big gulp of beer and shook his head.

"Bris." She leaned forward, pressing her palms flat on the table. "I don't understand. You speak volumes about anything and everything. You can talk for an hour about your love of ketchup. And yet whenever I ask about what happened in Haven, you clam up. It's suspicious."

He backed as far away from her as possible and crossed his arms, his eyes flitting toward the door. Definitely uncomfortable. "Do I?"

She nodded.

"I just don't want to talk about it."

She sipped on her margarita, tasting the tang of the salt. "You said that. And you also said that you're never going back."

He nodded. "True. I'm not."

46

"And so . . ."

He pressed his lips together.

She shrugged, and teased, "I'm sorry. You don't want me talking about the case. And yet we can't talk about that either. So what did you want to talk about?"

"I just wanted to have a good time. And neither of those subjects qualify," he said with the frown deepening on his face. His voice was hollow, distant. "But fine. We can talk about the case. What do you think? You think those girls on the reservation might be the key?"

She stared at him. It was really so bad that he really couldn't talk about it? What in the world was he hiding that was so terrible?

And clearly, he was disturbed by her bringing it up. She felt guilty for attempting to. So much for having a good time. The light-hearted mood was definitely broken, and there was no way of getting it back. So she reached into her purse and pulled out the file. "The two victims who were strangled on the reservation had both gone to Pierre a couple nights before their death. One went to a concert, one was a fast food delivery driver who traveled up and down the highway."

He pulled the files to him and studied them. "And Jessie and Marie also were in Pierre, prior. So we're thinking the murderer might've followed them from there?"

"It's possible. It's worth looking into, don't you think?"

"Yeah . . . but why the change from strangling to smothering?"

"Maybe he just uses what he finds around—if there was a knife, he'd use that. Or maybe he brought a rope with him, the first two times, but with Jessie, he forgot it. Found that using a pillow worked just as well. Decided he liked it, and would continue that way."

Michael stroked his chin. "So he's experimenting as he goes along, deciding what works best?"

"You know as well as I do that even when we profile these killers, they always manage to break out of the mold in surprising ways."

"And how," he mumbled, downing his beer and motioning to the waitress for another one.

She watched him, wondering if he was drowning his sorrows because she'd brought up his past. All the more, she felt herself wondering about it. It didn't make sense. She was a normally reserved, private person, and she'd told him about her closet skeleton. Why wouldn't he do the same?

More and more, it made her wonder if that smiling façade was just a thick mask to disguise a broken man. And more and more, she had to wonder if she really knew Michael Brisbane as well as she thought she did.

Did it matter? Why was she letting that nag her? She had a real case to solve.

That was probably why she felt herself growing more and more annoyed. Not just that he wouldn't share with her, like she'd done with him—but that it was making her think about him too much. She didn't need him and his problems occupying space in her head when she needed to devote every brain cell she could to this case.

"All right," she said, pushing those thoughts of Michael's past away. "So here's our agenda. First we find a hotel to stay at tonight."

"And not Horror Movie House."

"Clearly. Then, tomorrow, we'll lay out all the files and try to see where they connect. Sound good?"

Before he could reply, their food came. They dug in, eating silently for a few moments, and the longer the silence stretched on, the guiltier she felt. He was right. He'd wanted a few hours away from the doom and gloom, and she hadn't even been able to do that. She *was* a stick in the mud.

"I'm sorry," she said quietly.

Still chewing, he took a sip of his beer. "For what? It's not your fault."

"It is! You're right. I can't relax."

"Apparently, I'm the one who can't, this time," he said with a shrug. "But I guess this isn't the time to relax. Not with a murderer on the loose, who might be out there, choosing his next victim as we speak."

She put her fork down, her appetite lost. "Yeah. That's always in the back of my mind. But then again, what else can we do? We don't have enough to narrow down as to where he might strike next. Even if we spent all night driving up and down the highway, we'd probably miss him."

"Yeah." He let out a sour laugh. "Well, so much for a nice night out."

She smiled sadly. "I told you, I ruin things! I always put damper on everything."

"Nah, I think we're both just not in the mood. Because of the case. Maybe next time you'll take me up on the offer when we're between cases?"

She nodded. "Yeah. That sounds good."

He nodded and motioned to the waitress for the check. "So let's go get some sleep. Then tomorrow we'll look at this case with fresh eyes."

CHAPTER NINE

So much for getting home before dark.

The sun had fully set as Vera Langley drove out of Pierre, headed for her home in Norvander.

She'd meant to leave earlier. She really had. The South Dakota Farm Association's annual conference had been over at five, and it was only an hour's drive to her farmhouse outside of the capital. But Ed had picked a restaurant right on the river, and she'd been starving.

Plus, Ed had begged her, and he was the boss. A silver tongue, just like the mighty Missouri, glowing outside their window overlooking downtown Pierre. He'd spent most of the time talking to her about her future in his company. She'd only been working for TAYS-T, his pet food business, for three months-- she was in procurement—but he seemed to think she had the intellect and savvy to run the whole operation in a matter of years. He'd wanted to send her to their overseas operations in France and China.

Not so bad for a twenty-two-year-old who'd never been to college.

Take that, she wanted to say to her boyfriend, George, who always told her those online business courses she took were worthless.

Of course, one problem was that the liquor had been flowing freely, and she wasn't used to drinking much.

Now, as she drove south on I-86, she blinked away the double vision, and a horrible thought came to her. *Oh, I hope I don't get pulled over. If I get a DUI, I'll be in so much trouble!*

She checked the speedometer to confirm her speed was okay, then tried to focus her eyes on the lines ahead. It was now fully dark, and of course, George had been texting her, wondering if she'd gotten back home yet. He was always keeping tabs on her, especially since they didn't live together. He was the jealous type.

But he had nothing to worry about with Ed. Ed was old enough to be her father. Sure, he'd gotten a bit close over dinner, but that was just the liquor. He really wanted her to succeed. He told her that he saw her as his protégé, and that he wanted her to go far in the pet food business.

And she could just see it now. CEO of her own business, at the age of thirty. She wouldn't have to rent an apartment—she could buy a mansion, right on the river. She could just imagine waking up to the sight of the river, every morning.

Of course, she'd dump George. He was cute, and they'd been sweethearts all through high school, but he had no faith in her whatsoever. He was perfectly happy working at Tony's Farm Supply, as a cashier, making minimum wage. She got the feeling he would be completely happy if she stayed home, barefoot and pregnant, once they got married.

And live on his minimum wage salary their whole lives?

She cringed at the thought. She didn't even want kids. She wanted more. Much more.

She was so deep in thought that she nearly missed the sign that said: STOP AND PAY TOLL $1 ONE MILE AHEAD.

She saw it as she was passing it, and it immediately struck her sober. A dollar. Sure, she was making good money at TAYS-T, but it all went straight into her bank account. No one carried cash around, these days.

That's why when this stupid toll was announced a few months ago, anyone and everyone complained. She'd even told George that it was going to be a shitshow. They didn't allow anyone to use the electronic toll system, as they did in civilized states like Minnesota. This was cash or else.

She scrambled, taking her foot off the gas slightly, fishing around in the cup holders. All she found there was a quarter. Grabbing her purse from the front seat, she felt in the change pocket of her wallet. All she had there was another fifty cents. She rooted around the floor of her giant purse, trying to scrounge up any change she could, but only came up with a stray button and a bobby pin.

"Oh, no," she muttered as toll plaza came into view. She slowed even more, digging between the seat cushions and praying she'd find something other than lint.

Her speed dropped to thirty-five, and then thirty, and finally, twenty. She was almost at the plaza, where it narrowed down to only one lane. Letting out a sigh, she advanced to the toll collector and smiled. "Hi," she said, depositing her seventy-five cents into his hand.

He counted it and shook his head. "This isn't enough."

"I know. I'm a quarter short. But couldn't you just . . ."

The man shook his head solemnly. "Please proceed to the shoulder."

Her eyes widened. "Are you serious?"

"You heard me," he muttered, pointing with great force, like a drill sergeant. "Shoulder. Now."

She didn't like his militaristic attitude. He thought he was General Patton and not some middle-of-nowhere toll collector. *Over one freaking quarter?* she thought, but sighed and pulled to the side of the road, anyway.

Then she blew into her hand and sniffed. She didn't smell too much like the Malibu Bay Breezes she'd consumed at the restaurant, did she? The last thing she needed was for this guy to summon the police.

All over twenty-five cents! She smoothed her hair and skirt and checked her reflection in the rear-view mirror. She looked terrified.

When she powered down the window of her compact car, the toll collector was coming toward her. She couldn't make out much of him, other than his slow, practiced gait, because he was shining a flashlight into her eyes.

"Do I have to remind you that it is a felony to try to skip out on tolls?" the man said in a gruff voice.

"I know, I wasn't trying to—"

He held out a big palm, clearly uninterested in her excuses. "License?"

She blinked and reached for her purse. "Am I going to get a ticket?"

"I am going to make a copy of your license, and a bill for the toll plus a penalty fee of fifty dollars will be sent to you. I advise you not to delay in paying it."

She'd found her license, but now, her jaw dropped. "Fifty dollars? But it's—"

"Doesn't matter. That's the law," he said, taking her license and reading it over. "Vera Langley. Sit right here and don't move."

Don't move? Really? Was she supposed to freeze like a statue? She wanted to call George. But George would probably tell her how stupid she was for forgetting the toll. Instead, she watched the toll collector step across the traffic lane to the toll house in her side-view mirror, feeling more and more miserable. *Aren't you a freaking ray of sunshine? Jerk.*

Fifty dollars, for a stupid mistake. Over a freaking quarter! If she'd remembered, if she'd just asked Ed for the dollar, there would be no problem. But fifty dollars? She'd have to work all morning to make that kind of money. Forget splurging on that designer purse she'd seen online. Maybe Ed would let her work through her lunch break . . .

An idea came to her. She always went to the gym on her lunch break, since it was a little place just around the corner, and when she was there, she bought herself a bottle of water, so she liked to have change with her. She reached behind the seat and pulled out her gym bag, then felt inside. Immediately, she pulled out a folded wad of singles. "Ah!"

The toll collector was coming back. This time, she straightened and smiled victoriously. "I found it!" she said, waving the dollar in front of the beam of flashlight. "Here it is."

He stared down at it for a moment, and then said, "I'm sorry."

He handed her the dollar back, and the license. She looked at it in confusion. "Wait . . . what?"

"It's already been recorded in our system. I'm sorry. There's nothing you can do, except make sure you always have the money handy when you travel on this road."

"What? I do have the money! So you're saying I owe it, even though I—"

"That's right. Are you going straight home from here to Linbrook Avenue?"

She realized he was staring at the copy he'd made of her license. "Yes."

"Good. Then you shouldn't have any other tolls in your way." He patted the top of her car. "Please proceed and be safe."

He turned and headed back to the toll plaza, leaving her steaming in anger. How was that legal? The state had basically just stolen fifty dollars from her. She wondered if George had any advice.

No, not George. Ed. Ed knew everyone in this state, it seemed. He'd probably know a way to get her out of it.

But for now, she'd just have to deal with it. At least she wasn't being arrested for DUI.

Shifting her car into drive, she checked her side-mirror, making sure the lane was clear, and pulled out, heading toward home.

CHAPTER TEN

It turned out that Easy Rest Hotel *was* the only hotel in a fifty-mile radius.

Rylie really searched, but their only other option was to drive into Pierre and find a hotel there. But that would've put them at a disadvantage if they planned to drive south to the Indian reservation. So, in the end, they drove up the hill and grabbed their things from the back of Michael's truck.

As he slammed the door, Michael said, "I wouldn't take a shower tonight, if I were you."

She gave him a confused look. "Why? Mold?"

"You might peel back the shower curtain and find a guy dressed like his mother."

Oh, right. She'd almost forgotten. Good ol' Michael, reminding her. She was tired, but she wondered if she'd be able to sleep, thinking of that.

They found Fiona, still sitting on that same stool behind the desk, finishing up her Sudoku puzzle.

"You're back!" she said brightly when they arrived.

"Hi," Rylie said, managing a smile as she lugged in her duffle. "Yep, we're back."

"Not many hotels around here, huh?" she said with a smile. "I've heard that before. Do you need a room this time, or do you have more questions?"

She looked over at Michael. "*Two* rooms, please."

"Sure thing!" Fiona grabbed two keys from the pegs. From the location of the pegs, Rylie assumed that the two rooms were on the opposite end from the cabin where Jessica was murdered. They handed over the credit card information, and once they were done, Fiona said, "Do you need me to show you to your rooms?"

"I think we've got it," Michael said.

They went out to the back of the house, where Rylie noticed that they were the only guests there. If there were any travelers in the area, they'd obviously found somewhere else to stay. She took her key and went to the first cabin. "Sleep tight," she called to him as he trudged slowly to his door.

"You, too," he said, and then looked up. "Oh. And don't forget. Your door doesn't lock automatically."

She smiled. So that's why he was walking so slow. He was trying to make sure she got in okay. "Thanks for the reminder. I've got it."

The key was old and stuck in the lock. As she tried to open it, he said, "Hey."

She looked up to find him staring at her in the darkness. "Yes?"

He let out a big sigh and walked over to her, jumping from his porch to hers. "Look. I'm sorry if I shut you down about my past. I'm just not ready to—"

"No, it's okay," she said lightly. "I shouldn't have pried. You don't have to tell me."

"I know, but you told me about what happened to you," he said, rubbing the back of his neck anxiously. "And well—"

"It wasn't a tit for tat thing, Bris. You don't ever have to tell me, if you don't want to. But if it's ever getting in the way of your job . . . then maybe I can help you," she said honestly. "That's why I told you about my past. Because it was getting in the way of my job. And because I thought you could help me. And you did. You found that necklace."

He nodded, but he seemed unconvinced. "Yeah, I guess . . ."

It was on the tip of her tongue to tell him about Griffin Franklin, the man who the evidence had led to, but she wasn't sure he needed to know. She'd already involved him enough. This was her fight. "Good night."

She opened the door, went inside, and closed it, thinking about the damage he must've endured. What could've happened to him.

Then she shook it away and double-locked the door, using the chain and everything. It didn't matter. She had other things to worry about right now. Right now was all about the case. And if he wanted to keep his past buried, it was probably a good thing.

She threw her bag on the bed and went to the bathroom. Sure enough, there was a plain white shower curtain there, but she wasn't going to let that deter her. She ran the water, stripped out of her clothes, and took a nice, hot shower.

No disturbances, thank goodness.

Then, wearing an oversize t-shirt and towel in her hair, she went to the bed, turned on the television to some mindless reality show, and spread out the files of the two cold cases in front of her.

They'd happened almost a year ago. Both girls had lived blocks apart on the reservation. They'd been friends, looked alike, and were the same ages. As she'd read before, Lydia Hook had gone to a concert with friends in Pierre. The report mentioned that she got home to her apartment at midnight, as the neighbors saw her arrive. But she'd been murdered sometime during the night.

The other, Carrie Summerfield, was a driver for fast food delivery and was used to driving up and down the highway. In the report, the police had spoken to her mother, who said that she'd had an altercation with someone who had failed to pay, and then followed her down the street and harassed her the day before.

The women were the same age, but not the same physical type. Though the two women had lived rather close to one another, the others lived pretty far away. It was maddening, trying to make some kind of connection that tied them all together. Each time she thought she had one, she'd look at one of the four and realize it wasn't a connection at all.

Maybe they weren't connected, after all.

She sighed and looked up at the ceiling. Thoughts of Michael began to intrude. For a moment, she wondered what he was doing. Was he sound asleep, without a care in the world? Or was he more like she was? She could never fall asleep easily, and when she did, she always had nightmares. Did he have nightmares about his past, too?

Stop thinking about him.

She shoved the thoughts away and flipped through the files again. This time, as Rylie paged through, she noticed another thing all of the women shared, besides having driven on I-86.

They all lived alone.

Rylie gnawed on her lip. How did the killer know they lived alone? It wasn't like the crime scenes were proximate to one another, except for the two on the reservation. In fact, there was a fifty-mile gap between the reservation and Sweeten, where Marie's body was found.

Once again, I-86, the Highway Thru Hell, linked all the murders.

Maybe that was just because it was one unlucky road.

Or maybe it was something more.

56

Rubbing her hands together, she grabbed her phone and texted Beaker, the resident FBI tech-geek. Though barely out of school, he was a whiz when it came to computers and hunting down valuable data. Sometimes it seemed like there was nothing the kid with the fire-red hair and freckles couldn't do. *Hey, Beek, do you think you can round up credit card receipts, cell phone records, etc., to give me an idea of where four victims were prior to their murders?*

A moment later, he responded: *You do know it's midnight, right?*

She smiled. The kid was never far from technology, even during sleeping hours. *And yet, you're up, and on your computer. I know YOU.*

Touché. Give me the names and addresses.

She typed them in and sent them to him. He replied at once. *Give me a few hours. I'll see what I can dig up.*

Setting her phone aside, she willed herself to buckle down and read more, but her eyelids became heavy, and she yawned. The voices of the people on television seemed to stutter and halt, and she caught herself nodding off as her head drooped to her chin.

Finally, she gave in. She set aside the files and sunk into her pillow.

Moments later, she was in a campground, running among the trailers, playing hide and go seek with her sister. A couple years older, Maren had always been faster and better at hiding. She dipped easily between the different vehicles, her waist-length, shiny dark hair bouncing between her diamond-sharp shoulder blades.

"Catch me! Rylie! Bet you can't!" the girl taunted in a sing-song voice.

"I can! I will!" Rylie shouted, pounding the dirt clumsily in her flip flops as she took off after her.

Kiki was there, too. Rylie's best friend almost from birth, the two of them were peas in a pod. Where her own sister was almost her opposite, in a lot of ways, Kiki and Rylie shared a mind. When out of breath, they stopped, looking around helplessly, and Kiki tugged on Rylie's sleeve. She pointed to a shadow, swaying, of someone on the other side of the nearest trailer, and whispered, "You go around that way. I'll go around the other way. We'll catch her that way."

"Good idea," Rylie whispered, and the plan was set in motion.

Carefully, she crept around to the back of the trailer, which was hooded in shadow. She at least expected to see Kiki there, since that was part of the plan. But there was nothing but weeds.

57

"Run!" That voice belonged to Rose, Kiki's mother. It sounded frantic, panicked, yet Rylie couldn't see the woman anywhere. She turned to the direction of the disembodied voice, seeking out its source, when clouds suddenly appeared overhead and thunder boomed. "Run!"

But she was fastened in place. Everything seemed to be at a standstill, except for the driving rain falling around her. She tried to move, to call out for help, but nothing worked. It was as if she was encased in cement.

And then she realized the storm clouds above her were not storm clouds at all. It was instead the shadow of an enormous, hooded man, so big that he blocked out everything else in her vision.

Her eyes trailed up his faded blue jumpsuit, to his grizzled, hardened face and two coal-black eyes, like fathomless pits that bore into hers.

It was Griffin Franklin, the man she'd only seen in articles, the killer of all those women in North Dakota. He opened his mouth to reveal decayed, black teeth, and smiled as he said, "I took your sister. And you'll never get her back."

Then he reached for her, but again, she could not move. She could only stand and shake in horror as his fingers curled around her arm like tentacles . . .

Rylie woke with such a start that she sat up, stick-straight, in bed. She looked around at the plain white walls of the cabin. The television was tuned to some rerun of an old sitcom, canned laughter rolling through the silence. The light beside her bed was still on. Had she forgotten to turn it off?

Probably. She was always doing things like that.

The first thing she did was check her phone. Nothing yet from Beaker. Though it felt like ages since she'd texted him, it had actually only been an hour ago. He was good, but he wasn't a miracle worker.

She grabbed the remote and switched off the television, then turned off the light, leaving herself in darkness. Looking around in the almost black, a small slice of moonlight sending a square of white light onto the comforter of her bed, she thought again about her nightmare.

Then she thought about all those hidden dangers, lurking everywhere, even when they were least expected. She wondered whether somewhere, out there in the dark, the killer was preparing to strike again.

Then she turned the light back on, and rolled over, reminding herself, again and again, that some things were beyond her control. Tomorrow, they'd need to start out early if they were going to put Beaker's information to good use.

CHAPTER ELEVEN

Vera Langley finally pulled into her apartment complex in the town of Norvander at a little bit after one in the morning.

She was still reeling from the fifty-dollar ticket she'd be getting in the mail, all because she'd been unable to pay the toll. She'd spent most of the time grumbling under her breath, thinking of exactly what strong words she'd use in a letter to the highway commission. If Ed couldn't help, that seemed like the next logical step.

When she stepped out of her car, the parking lot was full, but quiet. Most of the lights in the neighboring apartments were off. She walked down a path and around a corner, to a corridor where her apartment was located. It was dark, and all the lights on the pathway were off.

"That's totally unacceptable," she muttered. She'd spoken to the superintendent half a dozen times over the past few months, trying to get them fixed. But had he? No. She'd nearly twisted her ankle on the path a few days ago, stumbling around in her heels in the dark.

Rummaging through her bag for her keys, she opened the door to her apartment and stepped inside, flipping on the lights. Even with the lights on, the apartment seemed cold and empty. George had said something about moving in together, so they could save money for the wedding, but she wasn't so sure. He still lived with his parents, for God's sake. He had no ambition whatsoever. Lately, it seemed like her star was taking off, while he was at a standstill, content to relive his high school glory days.

They'd had this argument before. She'd made it perfectly clear that he needed to contribute his share before she'd consider saying yes to his proposal. But had he gone out and gotten a good job with benefits? Nope, he was still working that dead-end slog, where he'd be making minimum wage for the rest of his life.

Was that the kind of future she wanted? Hell, no. Maybe it was time to end things with him, once and for all.

She looked around her apartment. It was one of the nicest addresses in Norvander, brand new, with modern fixtures and high-end furniture.

All of it was because of her. He'd wanted to move in here, but she was the one putting it off.

Nights like this, she almost caved. It would be nice to have someone to come home to.

But that was the only thing he was good for. Everything else about him annoyed her. From the way he picked his teeth at the dinner table to how he constantly leered at other women when they went out—he wasn't subtle or cultured in the least. Sometimes she wondered how she'd ever found him cute in high school.

It was the damn football uniform. Most guys look adorable in those tight pants. But since then, he'd even let his body go, growing quite the belly for a guy who wasn't yet twenty-five.

No, there was very little about the old George that she recognized now.

Sighing, she dropped her keys on the granite kitchen counter, kicked off her shoes, and went to the fridge. She opened it and pulled out a bottle of water, then shook a couple of capsules of acetaminophen from the bottle on the shelf over the sink onto her palm.

Downing them, she stretched, realizing how hot and stuffy it was. There was something wrong with the circulation in this apartment building. She'd thought it from the start. Sometimes, it was hard to breathe. She'd told the super about it, a week after she moved in, but he explained that was the trade-off in moving someplace where everything was brand new—there was still a lot of construction dust settling, which could interfere with circulation. He told her he always changed the filters in the HVAC, every week, but that eventually it would get better.

It hadn't, yet. She coughed, then took another sip of water.

Then she trudged down the hall, toward her bed.

A moment--or perhaps hours--later, she woke to the sound of a peculiar rattling, coming from down the hall. It sounded like someone was rolling something across the hardwood floors.

The sound faded, and she closed her eyes, sure she'd imagined it.

Then she realized she was in bed, and couldn't remember ever having gotten there. Things flitted through her mind—memories of the drive home, that stupid toll collector, pulling into her spot—but she couldn't remember anything that had happened after that. How had she gotten to bed?

Dragging her hand down her side, she realized she was still wearing her work clothes. So it had been that kind of night. Right—she'd been at that dinner with Ed. And she'd been drinking.

She rolled over in bed and looked at the clock on the nightstand. It said 3:43. She blinked and realized she hadn't yet set the alarm for tomorrow. She usually woke up at five.

Five? Oh, God. I could sleep for another ten hours.

Now more awake, she grabbed for the clock and hastily set the alarm for 5:30. Ed would let her be a little late. During their conversation last night, he'd already said she was his favorite. And he was the one who'd kept her. He'd understand.

She set the clock down and lay back. She was just drifting off when she heard the sound again.

A rattling. This time, it seemed different. Louder. Closer.

Had she opened a window somewhere? Maybe the sound was coming from outside. But she couldn't remember. And no . . . the sound was too close, like almost outside her bedroom door.

Though sleep was calling to her, she pulled herself out of bed. She tripped over her skirt as she made her way to the door of her bedroom, listening. She followed the sound down the hall, toward the bathroom. There, the sound was horribly loud and jarring.

It was coming from the pipes. Someone in the complex had likely flushed a toilet or something.

"Not acceptable," she muttered, making a note to tell the superintendent about that problem, too, when she complained about the lack of lights outside.

The noise soon quieted again. Vera sighed and reversed direction. It wasn't right. The reason she'd rented this apartment in the newest complex in Norvander was because she'd hoped to avoid all these little problems—broken and worn things that constantly needed fixing. Since she'd expected her work life to be busy and time consuming, she needed everything associated with running her home to be worry-free.

A strongly worded complaint letter was definitely in order, now.

As she nestled into bed, the rattling started once more.

Just a pipe, somewhere in the building, she told herself, rolling over in bed and closing her eyes. *Someone is running a shower.*

But then she heard another sound. This time, it was different. A sharp crack.

Her eyelids fluttered open just in time to see a man in black, standing over her.

In a split second, he brought the pillow down on her face, blocking out all of her senses. The only thing she could feel was the fear, and the burn of the air, exploding in her lungs. Her limbs went numb, and she tried to fight, to scream, but she was too tired, and too weak to fight. She gave in easily, just as easily as she'd given in to sleep, only hours before.

CHAPTER TWELVE

When Rylie woke up that morning, the first thing she did was check for messages from Beaker.

Sure enough, she'd gotten one: *Sent it all to your email, boss.*

Excited, she'd opened her email to find files upon files, including a map of each woman's whereabouts, in the days prior to their murders.

That Beaker really does deserve a raise, she thought, rushing to get ready for the day. She couldn't wait to sink her teeth into the new information.

It was only as she was staring into the mirror, brushing her teeth, that the memory of her nightmare came back to her. Griffin Franklin, standing over her, telling her she'd never see Maren again. She had to wonder if her subconscious was trying to tell her something. Though she'd been in hiding and couldn't remember anything about two killers that had terrorized them that day . . . maybe she was blocking it out? Maybe she'd seen more than she knew.

Maybe her brain was trying to tell her that Franklin had been there, that day.

And if so, she *really* needed to talk to him.

Of course, it would take time. Kit hadn't sent her a peep since she'd put in her request to visit the prison, three days prior. It was probably too soon to bug her for an update.

Besides, she had other things to concentrate on. She pulled on her shoulder holster and blazer, fluffed her dark hair in the mirror, and stepped outside to find Michael, sitting on a rusting old lawn chair, on his porch, a folded newspaper in his lap. "Morning," he said, sipping from a Styrofoam cup.

"Good morning," she said, surprised to find him awake already. She was usually the one, pushing them out the door. "So I take it you didn't have any strange visitors with butcher's knives surprising you in the shower?"

"Nope, I made it out alive," he said, standing. Despite the early hour, he was meticulously dressed in his blazer and tie, not a hair out of place. The only lack of grooming she ever noticed on him was the dark stubble he accumulated by the end of the day, but that made him look better. Now, he was clean-shaven, and looked as though he'd had a full eight hours of sleep.

Unlike her. She'd only gotten four, at most. It was because of that nightmare. It probably served her right, for reading up on murder case files, right before bed.

He tucked the newspaper under his arm. "Coffee's in the front office, if you want some?"

"Sure," she said, and they walked together over to the farmhouse. As they did, she yawned.

"So you didn't sleep last night? Worried about the Psycho killer?" he asked.

"No, I was thinking about the *other* killer," she said as he opened the door for her to let her pass through. "The one we're currently tracking. I was going through the files last night."

"Find anything?"

Before she could speak, Fiona popped up from behind the counter. "Good morning!" she said to Rylie. "Hope you slept well! Coffee and donuts, fresh this morning!"

Rylie went to the large, metal tureen and filled a cup. "Yes. Thanks. Slept great."

"Will you be checking out today?"

She glanced at Michael, who shrugged. It'd been such a bear to find a local place, last night. "You know, I think we might just keep the rooms for another night, if that's okay?"

"Sure thing! You want housekeeping?"

Rylie shook her head. "We're good. But thanks." Then she turned to Michael and spoke in a low voice. "I didn't find anything specifically, but I did ask Beaker to send me over all the information he could compile on the victims' whereabouts prior to the crimes, so we could look it over."

"Good thinking," he said as they went outside. "So I guess we'll be looking that over?"

She nodded. "Well, I will. You'll be driving us to our next stop."

"Breakfast?" He pointed behind him. "Because I'm telling you, those donuts were as hard as rocks."

She rolled her eyes. "Fine. Whatever. But can we do something fast?"

"Yeah. I think we passed a fast food place on the way in."

They got into the car and he pointed his truck in the direction of the greasy spoon across the street. Meanwhile, Rylie started scrolling through the data Beaker had supplied. As he pulled into the lot, Rylie said, "Hey, this is interesting."

He pulled into a parking spot. "What is?"

"One of the two women from the reservation—Lydia Hook—and Marie Bottoms-- both stopped at the Gas-o-Rama in Sackville, the day before they died. Beaker found credit card receipts that show they both filled up with gas there."

"Sackville. Where's—"

"It's right outside of Pierre. I think we might have passed it last night when we were looking for a place to stay."

"Yeah?"

Michael made a move to cut the engine, but she said, "Wait. Don't you think we should . . ."

He sighed and sat back against the chair. "You want to go there, now?"

She nodded, still scrolling through. "I don't see any indication that Carrie Summerfield or Jessie Vega did. But it's possible. They might have just paid in cash."

He stared at her, and she stared back, eyes pleading. Finally, he sighed. "So yeah . . . we're forgetting breakfast. Is that it?"

She smiled, and said in her sweetest voice. "Could we?"

He pressed his lips together, then grabbed his sunglasses from the center console and put them on. "I guess."

She checked and noticed that no one was using the drive-thru. She pointed at it. "We can compromise?"

"That's more like it." He pulled out and eased up next to the ordering board. "What do you want?"

"I guess . . . just get me a hash brown." Her stomach was starting to churn, as it usually did when she was antsy, following a case. The more she read, the more this seemed like the key they were looking for.

He ordered a giant heart attack on a biscuit, and two black coffees for the two them, as she continued to get lost, searching different threads for more connections. The Uber Driver, Carrie Summerfield, had been dozens of places over the past couple of days. The others, though, had mostly stuck to places right off of I-86. It made sense, considering they were all returning home from somewhere up north.

66

"I feel like somewhere along the line, all of these women must've run into our killer. But where? I have a good feeling about this gas station."

"All right, all right," Michael said, settling the two coffees into the cup holders between them. He grabbed his sandwich from the bag and took a bite, all the while managing to navigate onto the main road. Somehow, he managed to do all that with flair. "What am I taking? East? West?"

"East." She picked anxiously at her hash brown as they headed up the ramp to I-86 East. "Oh. Don't forget the dollar for the toll."

"Got it," he said, fishing a crumpled bill out of the change tray between them. He did this all while driving with his knees, since he had the sandwich in his other hand, and he had to slow his merge onto the road. "I'm so prepared I might as well be a boy scout."

She reached out and steadied the wheel. Luckily, the road was as empty as usual, even for near rush hour. "Focus, please."

"I have total focus," he said, grabbing the wheel. "Relax."

They were back to that again. *If I had a dollar for every time you have to remind me to chill out, I could retire from the force a rich woman.*

"All right. It's the next exit," she told him. "After the toll."

He slowed to hand his dollar to the collector. "Good morning!" he said to the woman there.

"Morning to you," she said with a smile. She was a lot nicer than the one who'd been there, earlier, that was for sure. "Safe travels!"

Michael mock saluted her and powered up the window, then steered to the right lane to take the Sackville exit, finished off his sandwich, and licked his fingers clean. "Let's hope someone here remembers something about those girls."

CHAPTER THIRTEEN

The thought that someone would remember those girls was a long shot.

Rylie knew that the moment the trees parted and they drove down the exit. The Sackville Gas-o-Rama was a massive complex, with at least twenty pumps situated in an L around a sprawling convenience store, gift shop, and sit-down diner.

Her jaw dropped as they got closer to it. It looked brand new, and despite the fact that they hadn't seen many cars on the road at all, the place was a madhouse. It was crawling with people coming in and out, swarming like ants on a cookie. Michael had to swerve to miss a sportscar that was trying to navigate next to one of the pumps.

"I thought once we got out of the Black Hills, there wasn't much to see in South Dakota. I guess they're expecting this place is going to get built up in the next few years?" Michael suggested.

"Looks like it's already doing pretty well," she said, noticing another sign. It said, *OLD WEST VILLAGE! ONE MILE AHEAD.* "Oh, that's what it is. It's for that amusement park up there."

"This place looks like an amusement park in itself," he said, pointing to the giant frog statue, which must have been the gas station's mascot, standing at the entrance. "They're doing a business."

"Yeah, but in a place like this, who is going to notice two women?"

He sucked in his cheeks. "Yeah. Well, doesn't hurt to try, I guess."

It was so crowded that they had to wait for a parking spot. By the time they found one and pulled in next to the convenience store, Rylie was more anxious than ever. She yanked off her seatbelt and hopped out of his truck almost before Michael came to a full stop. Then, weaving through the throng of people, she slipped through the sliding doors.

Inside was just as crowded as out. There was a long line of people waiting to be seated at the restaurant, another long line of people waiting to have their deli orders made, and then another at the main cash registers. Rylie looked around in sheer wonder for a moment. The poor workers here looked like they hardly had a chance to breathe.

She noticed a woman restocking the Grab & Go case with sandwiches, and said, "Oh, miss? Can I ask you a question?"

The woman looked over at her for a moment and said, hurriedly, "Hmm?" as she continued to load the case.

Someone nudged her from behind and reached into the case to grab a sandwich. Another person lunged between them and took one. It seemed like people were grabbing the sandwiches as fast as the woman could load them.

"I'm Special Agent Wolf from the FBI." She reached for her credentials, but it didn't seem like the woman cared. "I just wanted to ask you if you'd seen someone."

The lady snorted. "I've seen a lot of people. But I doubt I'd remember any of them. When was this?"

"Couple nights ago?"

Just then, there was a crash, and a scream, and a baby started crying, somewhere in the back of the store. They both looked past the aisles to see a giant spilled mess on the ground. Someone had knocked over a coffee carafe.

"Oh, just perfect!" The woman groaned and looked at Rylie, shaking her head. "Look, I don't even work nights. If you go through those doors, the manager could give you a look at the security footage."

She rushed off and a moment later, Rylie saw her making her way toward the scene of the accident with a bucket and mop. Meanwhile, people swerved around her in all directions. Rylie had to move out of the way of the Grab & Go case before she was trampled. By the time she was able to get free, the case was nearly empty.

*

Twenty minutes later, Rylie emerged from the back room to find an even bigger crowd. Only a few minutes of viewing the security footage had produced a lot of disappointment—the output had been so grainy that she hadn't been able to see a thing.

"Wolf!"

The low, loud call rose over the general din. She looked across the store and saw Brisbane, standing out among all the other customers, because of his height and formal attire. He snapped his fingers at her from the center of the snack food aisle, where it didn't look like he was faring much better. "Over here!"

She fought the tide of bodies in order to get over to him, and let out a sigh of relief when she was finally in a safe spot where she wouldn't be jostled. "This place is insane," she mumbled. "The security footage is worthless, and of course, no one had seen anything. They barely have time to breathe, much less notice anything."

"Well, this kid has," Michael said, moving slightly to the right to reveal a skinny kid with a mess of red curls. He was crouched next to a cardboard box and loading items as fast as he could, into the rack.

Now it made sense why Michael was just standing there—he was shielding the kid so he wouldn't get trampled by the hordes. "He did?"

Michael nodded. "Hey. Skip. Tell my partner what you told me."

Skip popped up. He was tall and skinny and couldn't have been more than sixteen or seventeen. He was wearing an apron with that same cartoon frog on it, and a red visor. "Hi. Yeah. I saw those women."

Rylie blinked, surprised. "Are you sure?"

He nodded. "Yep. I usually work nights after school. I remember them because they were *hot*. Like, smoking. One of them—that one—" He pointed to the photograph of Jessie. "She was wearing this top where I could see all of her—"

Michael nudged him. "Okay, okay, enough, kid. We're not interested in that. Did you say anything to them?"

He grinned. "That girl? Yeah. She came in and asked me if I had any frosted donuts, and I went in the back and looked for her. I found them, and she hugged me. She smelled like apples. She said she didn't know how to thank me, so I asked her out. Figured it was worth a shot."

Michael raised an eyebrow. "And what did she say?"

"No," he said with a shrug. "Obviously. She said she wasn't into robbing the cradle but that in another couple of years, who knows?"

He grinned, but it slowly faded when Rylie asked, "Did you see her with anyone? Did you notice her talking to anyone, or anyone watching her?"

"No . . . I mean, all the guys in the place were looking at her. She was hot. I watched her go out and she got in her car and drove away. She was alone." He swallowed as his eyes darted between the agents' grave faces. "Wait . . . did something happen to her?"

Rylie didn't answer that. "And you said you saw this woman?" she said, pointing to the picture of Marie Bottoms on Michael's phone.

"Yep. Saw her, too." His upper lip turned up slightly, almost in disgust. "She was hot but she had an attitude. I think something was bothering her. When she came in, she was on the phone, and I heard her say something about a divorce."

Until that moment, Rylie had been questioning whether he'd met these women at all or if he was just spinning a yarn for the fun of it. But at that, she realized he was telling the truth. Marie Bottoms had traveled up to Wisconsin to meet her family, and that was when she'd decided to get the divorce lawyer. This kid couldn't have known that unless he'd actually seen her. "Was she with anyone?"

He shook his head. "She just came in, paid for her gas, got a coffee, and left. She seemed like she was in a rush, wherever she was going."

Rylie glanced at Michael, who seemed proud of himself for uncovering this new witness. This meant that both of the recent cases had been here. She said, "Did you show him the pictures of the women from the cold cases?"

He nodded, and Skip said, "That's what I was just telling him. They happened months ago, right? I wasn't here, then. In fact, this whole place wasn't here then."

"It wasn't?"

"Nah. It was a little ma and pa shop, had only one pump out front." He smiled. "I know because I live down the road, in the trailer park on the other side of the highway. When the Warners retired and sold the station, it was a big deal."

"The Warners?"

He nodded. "Yeah. They owned most of this area. They're the owners and my neighbors in the park. Nice folks. She died a couple months ago, but Mr. Warner still lives there. You can ask him?"

Rylie reached for a pen and paper in her bag. "Yeah, can you tell us where this trailer park is? On the other side of the highway?"

"Sure can. It's called Mesquite Acres. I'm right next to his trailer."

"Thanks," she said, pocketing the information.

"You've been very helpful, kid," Michael said, giving the boy a fist-bump, then handing him his card. "You call me if you think of anything else, all right?"

The kid read the card and said, "Wow, is this for real? FBI. Wow. I didn't even know you guys came to armpits like this. Thought you were too busy protecting the president and stuff."

"That's Secret Service." Michael gave him a thumbs-up. "Take it easy, now, okay?"

The kid grinned after them, and they managed to get out of the store without any major difficulty. "So that's two at least that were in the same place, and you have a credit card slip, you said, that showed Lydia Hook went there?"

"Yeah. Well, Beaker plotted it on the map but he didn't say it had changed hands in the meantime." When she slid into the passenger seat of the car, she fished out the paper and said, "Well, I guess we know our next stop."

"All right, hang on," he said, trying to find a break in the traffic behind him so he could pull out. "Let's go talk to Mr. Warner."

CHAPTER FOURTEEN

Bill Matthews wasn't happy.

The Special Agent in Charge of the FBI's Seattle unit was never happy when things didn't go his way. He didn't like being played.

But now, it seemed like Cooper Rich was definitely yanking his chain.

And he'd never been happy, where a single person was concerned.

Her name was Rylie Wolf. His former underling, she'd made his life a living hell for far too long, until he'd enlisted the help of his father, Deputy Director Jerry Matthews, to ship Wolf off to the hinterland. After that, he'd given himself a pat on the back, sure he'd never hear from her again.

He'd been wrong.

Since landing in the newly created force designed to stop crime along the I-86, Highway Thru Hell corridor, she'd made a bit of a name for herself. Not only had she found herself embroiled in a number of high-profile cases, she was labeled "instrumental" in solving them.

That had been enough to burn his biscuits. But now, there was more.

He'd thought that by enlisting Rich, he could find some dirt to help speed her demise. Rich had been her best friend in the unit. He knew her secrets. So he'd sent him out to see what she was up to. To spy.

But maybe he'd been too optimistic, thinking that he could force Rylie Wolf's best friend in the unit to help him bury her. Because so far? It'd been the better part of three weeks, and nothing had been done. In fact, she'd gone on to solve another big case. There was a photograph of her, in some throwaway Midwest newspaper, with a caption that read, *Highway Hero.*

Swallowing back the bile in his throat, he opened up the text exchange he'd had with Rich last week:

Bill Matthews: Her sister was murdered?

Cooper Rich: Yeah. I think. Or kidnapped. Like twenty years ago. But she's always been looking for who did it.

Bill Matthews: I think I can use that.

And he thought he could. He'd thought, for the first time, he'd be able to silence the thorn in his side, Rylie Wolf, for good.

The question was, how?

Again, he pulled up the article he'd found on the case, dated twenty years ago. It hadn't taken much legwork, but it did provide a lot of insight into the Rylie Wolf he knew:

STORY CREEK, WY – Three travelers were murdered and a 12-year-old girl was kidnapped from an RV park early Saturday morning.

Police were called to the scene by another RV owner, who was in the area and alerted to the crime by a 9-year-old girl who was in the party, and unharmed. Police say two women and their three children were staying in the park, when a person or persons unknown shot three of the victims once in the head and kidnapped the 12-year-old girl.

The kidnapped girl is about five feet tall and 90 pounds, with long dark hair and brown eyes. She is believed to be wearing a red tank top and jean shorts. Police are asking anyone who may have seen her to call them.

The nine-year-old had been Rylie. He had sympathy for her. That had to have been a hell of a thing to go through. That kind of traumatic event had probably led to her career choice, and likely shaped her into the woman she was now—a bitter, stubborn, and downright difficult woman who was resistant to authority.

He'd been right. He'd always known something was wrong with her, with the way she took control of each case, employing unorthodox and sometimes costly methods in order to get her man. She didn't think.

But it was worse than that. With a history like hers, she was probably even more unstable than he'd thought. It was only a matter of time before she blew up and really hurt someone. What she needed was mental help, not to be an FBI agent. She was dangerous to society.

Now, how would he prove that?

He had to think of something. She had a way of weaseling out of trouble. He'd have to make it watertight, so there was no way she could escape.

A moment later, the man himself, Cooper Rich, walked past his office. "Rich!" he cried.

Rich had been back from his assignment for a couple days. He'd done as he'd been told, tracking his good friend Rylie down, seeing what she was up to. The last thing he'd seen, before he'd gotten on the

74

plane to come back home, was Rylie, digging around in a well for evidence. She was still trying to find her sister, apparently, after twenty years. If that wasn't dogged determination, he didn't know what was.

Cooper Rich loped into his office, looking even less thrilled to be talking to him than usual. He'd never gotten the impression Rich liked him, or even respected him, but he usually played nice. Now, he looked downright surly.

Like his good friend Rylie Wolf. Every time she'd walk into his office, he felt like she was gritting her teeth to keep from calling him a total ass. Sometimes, quite a few times, she couldn't find the restraint.

"Yeah?"

He managed a smile. "Just checking to see what you're working on since you got back."

Rich eyed him suspiciously. "The Ledge case. Remember? You put me on it."

He had. It was some bullshit boring job, tying up loose ends for an upcoming trial, that any agent could do blindfolded. "Yeah. How's it going?"

He shrugged. "Fine. Almost done. What else did you want?"

Of course, he'd wanted something else. And Rich was no idiot. He knew who it involved, too. It was time to drop the pretense. "Have you heard lately from Wolf?"

He shook his head. "Nothing of a professional matter."

Matthews stared at him, assessing what that meant. So they *had* had personal interaction, since then. He'd always had the feeling that their relationship wasn't strictly professional, and that maybe the two of them were banging when she was here. While it might not have been appropriate for two special agents, it would've only gotten Rylie Wolf a slap on the wrist and a firm talking to.

He wanted her to have so much more. He wanted Rylie Wolf to suffer.

"You know what she's up to?"

"Yeah, she said something about a case in South Dakota, the last time I talked to her."

He laced his fingers in front of him, on his desk. "Did she mention anything about that sister of hers that she was looking for?"

His face fell. "No. I didn't ask. She doesn't like talking about it. The only reason I knew about it to begin with was that the guys in the

75

office were saying something about it. That's it. I never spoke to her directly about it at all."

His eyes flitted to the article on his computer. He'd spent too much time looking into it as well, but the information online was spotty, since it had happened so long ago. "So you don't have any other details about it?"

"No . . ." He frowned. "What the hell do you want it for? Why can't you just admit that despite her rough edges, she's a good agent?"

Bill Matthews scoffed. "Because my devotion to the bureau is to make sure that it upholds its standards. And she's a danger. I really think she's a powder keg, about to blow, and I don't want to be the one blamed for inaction if something goes wrong." He pointed to the papers on his desk. "We have her here, acting out, indicative of her wrestling with personal demons . . . it's worrisome. Don't you think?"

Rich crossed his arms. "No. I don't think. Just . . . keep me out of it. Don't ask me to spy on her again."

He turned to leave but Matthews just laughed. He'd ask Rich. And Rich would go. Unlike Wolf, the man was a coward. He could be trained to jump when Matthews said jump.

"If I tell you to go, you'd better go. If I want you to spy on Rylie, you sure as hell will. If I tell you to show up in downtown Seattle in a chicken suit, you'd better well find a way to do it. Or else."

Rich had stopped to look back at him, his scowl deepening. He slinked out of the office, shoulders slumped, as if he knew he was beaten.

Matthews smiled. And if he needed Rich again, he'd use him, as many times as he needed to. He'd use every resource at his disposal to make sure Rylie Wolf got what was coming to her.

Disgrace. A vacation from the FBI.

Or maybe even a lengthy jail sentence.

Yes, he thought, smiling as his eyes flitted to the article once again. *I would like that very much.*

CHAPTER FIFTEEN

Mesquite Acres was a sprawling trailer park on the other side of I-86 from the equally massive gas station. Rylie plugged 1490 Mesquite into Michael's GPS, and the route took them past a sign, painted on metal, that had faded so dramatically by the sun that the name of the place could barely be seen, surrounded on each side by flat, dusty terrain and browned bushes. The park itself was surrounded by metal fencing, and there were perhaps fifty dilapidated motor homes situated within it, though there was room for at least ten times more. A collapsing swimming pool and wind-pummeled playground were vacant in the distance, and although faint, sloppily played chords from a guitar were audible, there was no sign of life to be found.

"Looks like a nice place," Michael mused, pulling in front of the first trailer they approached.

"Right." She got out of his truck and watched him do the same. "I'll be right back. You don't have to come in with me."

"It's hot out here. I'll come."

They climbed the decaying wooden steps and Rylie pressed the buzzer beside the screen door. In the shadows, she could see movement.

"Door's open," someone said in a throaty voice.

Inside, it smelled overwhelmingly of cigar smoke, mothballs, and spoiled milk. Brisbane scraped his head on the entryway, then touched his head gingerly to make sure no foreign substance had gotten on his hair. The lobby was furnished with ancient metal lawn chairs with seats of woven nylon. A wilting fern hung in one corner, and a ragged copy of a gun publication sat on one chair. Not much else. The kitchen was only two steps beyond that, and a door to the bedroom was a leap beyond. A worn sky-blue carpet, coated completely with lint and hair, ran throughout. There was a large brown stain splashed upon the wall, as if someone had mistakenly thought food could be art and thrown a bottle of cola there. Though she wasn't one to suffer from claustrophobia, Rylie's stomach began to churn.

A fat gray cat, bald in places and intent on greeting its new visitors, jumped onto a counter, about a foot from her nose. She gasped, and Brisbane put his hands reassuringly on her shoulders.

"Jumpy, aren't you?" he asked in her ear, so she could hear his smile.

She shrugged him away. "I don't like cats."

"You don't? What the hell is wrong with you?" When she looked at him sourly, he was grinning. He called, "Anybody home?"

From the bedroom door, a man with a walker appeared, moving unsteadily toward them. He was almost completely bald except for some long, rebel hairs reaching in every direction from his fair, polished, pockmarked head. His face was like dried fruit, his lips were almost entirely consumed by the black, toothless hole that was his mouth. His misshaped, thick body moved gracelessly, with each step a calculated labor

Michael, ever the health-minded person, looked at that freakish display, and his eyes leaked a little disgust. His actions though, were genuine Michael Brisbane. He went to the man's side and helped him into his chair, then knelt beside him. "Is there anything I can get you?"

"I'm not an invalid, boy," he snapped, pushing Michael's hand away. "How long you staying for?"

"Actually, we're here on another matter. Are you Mr. Warner?" Rylie asked.

"Yeah. If you're gonna try to sell me something, I already got everythin' I need."

"We're from the FBI. We wanted to ask you about a couple of people you might have seen at the gas station you owned, on the other side of the highway."

"I sold that place. Now it's that giant travesty. You saw it if you came off I-86. Looks like goddamn circus."

"Yes, but this would be a year ago?" Michael said.

He picked his nose, examined the material he discovered, and flicked it across the room. "Sit."

Glancing at Michael, Rylie slid her backside onto one of the chairs, trying to afford herself as little exposure as possible to it. Michael, who looked afraid to come in direct contact with anything at all, remained standing.

"I saw all kinds of weirdos there. No one ever came asking me about it before. Now, you're knocking down my door? What gives?"

She opened her mouth to speak, but then stopped and looked over toward Michael. His eyes were transfixed on something in the kitchen, behind a sink piled high with dirty dishes. It was a calendar from 1983, but that wasn't all. Rylie could see the peachy-white color of skin, and waves of hair, both blonde and brunette. Two women. She couldn't tell what they were doing to each other, but something told her that she didn't want to know.

"I wanted to ask you specifically about two women who might have stopped at your station about a year ago, before it closed down."

"A year ago?" He shook his head. "Can't help you."

"Well—"

"I wasn't working there then. Had my heart attack couple years before I sold the business. Marlon. He was working there."

"Marlon?"

"Yeah. I don't know much about him. He lives here, in the back of the park. He's a quiet guy, pays his money on time. Never gives me no opportunity to come over to his place lookin' after the rent. Now, he's a janitor, works nights. His girl was a waitress at some restaurant. Real pretty. She left him, though. Don't know where she went. Women, you know, always running around."

He smiled up at Michael as if they shared that understanding. Michael smiled back vacantly, seemed to realize he was leaning against a counter, and jumped straight up, standing at attention.

"Why ain't you sitting?" The old man barked at him. "Sit!"

"Yessir," Michael said, his voice cracking. He carefully, reluctantly planted his backside on the sofa beside Rylie.

He looked Michael over from head to toe. "You a fed?"

Michael nodded.

"They'll hire anyone these days." Warner turned his attention to Rylie and wiped a bit of ketchup from the corner of his crusty chin. "What else you want to know?"

Rylie paused for a moment, her mind blank. Michael spoke up. "Did he engage in any behavior you thought was unusual?"

He shook his head, the loose flesh under his chin jiggling. "Kept to himself, that's all."

"No odd habits?" Michael asked.

Rylie presumed this was a lost question because Warner was so odd, himself, he probably didn't find many things to be odd.

"Liked to shoot arrows and drink beer down by the playground. Made up his own target and would shoot arrows for hours and hours." He picked his nose again, this time wiping his new discovery on the leg of his worn sweatpants. "I yelled at him once cause he was shooting them too close to the kids."

Rylie took the reins. "What did he do when you yelled at him?"

"Didn't say nothing. Jus' took his stuff and moved over a little bit. Didn't throw a fit or nothing." He looked in the general direction of the kitchen and said, "Didn't need to worry about him hitting no kids though. He hit dead-center all the time, no matter how drunk he got."

"He was that good?" Michael asked.

"Better than good. He was perfect."

"And where does he live?" Rylie asked.

"Green trailer. Out back. Has the target in the front. Can't miss it."

Rylie had more questions, but Mr. Warner fell asleep, snoring like a lawnmower, before she could ask them. It was just as well. They had another lead, now.

Afterwards, Rylie and Michael walked around the park, looking for the trailer in question. The homes seemed all but empty; any children that Warner had mentioned must have been in school. The playground looked as though it hadn't been used for at least a decade, and Rylie hoped that was the case, since the rotting metal frame of the swing set and the broken glass in the sand looked like cases of tetanus, waiting to happen.

"I'm half-waiting for a tumbleweed to come by," Michael said, scanning the area. "A green trailer? I don't see one."

But it wasn't fifty feet from where they stood. They both noticed it at once, and Michael shouted, "Look!"

There, on a chain link fence beside the playground, was a wooden board. The sun had all but bleached the rings invisible, but there were a smattering of holes gracing it. Most were focused on the direct center of the board. They approached it cautiously, as if it were a poisonous snake, and Michael pointed at the trailer next to it.

"That's not green."

He was right. Rylie squinted, looking for any trace of green among the rust. There wasn't another trailer anywhere close. The small windows were all clouded with dirt, and one of the screens was held in with duct tape. "But that's got to be the place."

"All right," Michael said doubtfully, climbing the steps to the door. "Here goes not—"

Before he could say more, the door swung open and a man appeared, holding a bow, the tip of the arrow pointed right between Michael's eyes.

He seethed, "Get the hell out of here, unless you want me to split your head like a melon."

CHAPTER SIXTEEN

Michael slowly put his hands up, afraid to make any sudden moves. The man might've been attractive, once, but with his graying, receding hairline, and whiskered chin, he was showing signs of age. With his wild eyes, his dingy short-sleeve dress shirt half-untucked, his hair as mussed as if someone had just run all their fingers through it, the guy behind the screen door in the trailer looked *seriously* bonkers.

Behind the agent, on the ground, he heard Rylie scramble for her gun. "FBI! Drop it!" she shouted.

Unfortunately, the guy didn't even look at her. It was almost as if he hadn't heard her at all. He kept his aim trained right on Michael's head, one eye closed, his hand tight on the bowstring, ready to release it at any moment.

The words Mr. Warner said rang through his ears. *Better than good. He was perfect.* Very little comfort, considering his head was now the target, and he was barely two feet away.

"Marlon? I'm Michael Brisbane from the FBI. I just wanted to ask you some questions," he said quietly. "Can you drop your weapon?"

"No," the man muttered, his lips twisted in disgust. "I got nothing to say to you. You'd better leave."

"Drop. The. Weapon," Rylie said, behind him. "Now!"

This time, Marlon heard her. He swung the bow toward her. The moment he did, Michael thrust his arms out, grabbing the arrow and the man's arm. He succeeded in pulling the arrow out of the bow, and when the man struggled to land a quick punch, Michael easily overpowered him. The bow clattered to the floor as he got the man in a headlock and wrestled him to the floor.

As Michael pressed him, face first against the ground, he moaned. Rylie tried to hand him her cuffs, but he waved her off. This guy wouldn't be a problem, now.

"Listen, dude," Michael said, leaning forward to speak into his ear. "We just want to ask you some questions."

The man was still struggling to get up, but after a moment of having Michael's weight on his back, his face growing redder and redder, he managed to choke out. "Okay. Let me up."

"No funny business, you got it?"

"Yeah, yeah, yeah, I got it," he said, breathless.

Michael let go and grabbed him by his back collar, pulling him up to standing. He shoved him back into the trailer and deposited him on the first seat he could find, a black, lint-covered futon. The guy sat there obediently, waiting.

"Now, that's more like it," he said to him, looking down and straightening his tie, which had gone askew during the struggle. When it was straight, he looked around. Typical bachelor pad, with worn furniture and posters of nude women all over the walls. It smelled like old fast food and motor oil. "Why the hell are you attacking us?"

Marlon pressed his lips together. "I don't like no strangers. Always coming around trying to steal stuff from me. I don't like people in general."

"You live alone?"

Marlon nodded.

"You had a girlfriend, though?" Rylie asked, standing in the doorway, her brow wrinkling at the sight of one of his raunchier pieces of artwork.

"Yeah. She left," he said tonelessly, staring at the threadbare carpet between his spread legs.

"And when was that?"

He shrugged and picked on a loose thread on his sleeve. "Year ago? Two? Who knows? All I know is that the bitch left."

Clearly, he wasn't too torn up over the end of the relationship. "You worked at the gas station, right?"

He nodded. "Back then, yeah. Now I'm a night janitor at the school. What's this about?"

"I'm hoping you can tell me about these women," Rylie said, scrolling through her phone. She thrust the photographs of the two women under his nose. "They were supposedly at the gas station you used to work at, a year ago. Ring a bell?"

He only looked for a second, and when he blinked away, there was something new in his eyes. Pain? Fear? Whatever it was, he suddenly shifted uncomfortably and cleared his throat. "Never seen them before."

83

Michael didn't believe that. He'd looked too quickly, giving it such a perfunctory glance that he couldn't have possibly made a determination. "You sure? Look again."

"Naw." He shoved the phone away with a violent swipe of his hand. "I told you, I ain't seen them."

Michael leaned over and smiled at him. "Hmm. I think you're lying."

"I think he is, too," Rylie said, leaning against the door jamb and crossing her arms.

He bared his teeth. "If you gonna go on accusing me of something, I think I ought to have a lawyer, shouldn't I?"

"Do you have a lawyer, Mr. . . ." He frowned. "I'm sorry. What's your name?"

"Greef. Marlon Greef. And no, I don't."

Rylie pressed on, undeterred. "Are you telling me, Mr. Greef, that you never watch television? Turn on the news? Ever? Because I'm sure, if you had, you'd have seen these photographs before."

Now, it was definite fear in his eyes. "Uh. I had no idea. I mean, maybe I saw them."

"Okay, well, then," Rylie said. "Did you see them at the gas station? Because they were there."

He shook his head. "I don't remember. I think I saw them. It was a long time ago."

"And yet you do remember having seen them?"

"Yeah, but . . ." He threw his hands down on his thighs. Then he motioned to the phone and pointed to the picture of Lydia. "When I worked the gas station. I remember the one girl, this girl, coming in, getting pissed because the frozen drink machine wasn't working. I told her it'd been that way for months and wasn't nothing I could do about it. So she gave me shit. And then she bought a six-pack and left."

He shrugged as if that was enough.

"And the other?"

He pressed his lips together and swallowed a couple of times, as if he was having trouble getting something down. Something about this memory clearly pained him.

When he finally did speak, he said, "She was real chatty. Worked for one of those food delivery places. She was buying a couple of wine coolers for her dinner. Told me that she couldn't find the last address so they'd canceled the order, and she was gonna go home and eat it. It was like five burgers. I said, 'You gonna eat that all by yourself?' And she said she lived by herself. I told her I'd be right over, joking like, and she said, 'Nice try' and left. But she winked at me, and so. . ."

"And so?" Michael asked, leaning forward. When he didn't speak, he prompted, "And then what happened?"

He shrugged. "What do you mean? That's all. She left."

"You seemed like you were going to say more. She winked, and then . . ." Michael moved his hand in a circle as if to indicate the next logical event. "What?"

Marlon licked his lips. "Nothing. Uh, that was all. She drove away."

Rylie lifted her eyes to the ceiling, sighed dramatically, as she often did, and scoffed. "You really expect us to believe that?"

He swallowed, not meeting either of their eyes. "It's the truth. The God's honest truth." He crossed his heart. "I never saw those girls again."

Again, he looked down at his feet. *Liar,* Michael thought. And from the way Rylie was pacing, her movements tight and bothered, she felt it, too.

"So where have you been lately? You're a janitor at the school? Which school?" Brisbane asked. "The one across from the gas station?"

He nodded. "Sackville Elementary."

"At night?"

He nodded again.

Michael looked at Rylie to see if she was getting this. He'd been at the same gas station the two girls from the reservation had visited, and he'd worked across from the gas station when the other girls had visited it. That meant he'd been nearby all the victims. "Would it surprise you to know then that four women that have come to that gas station have been murdered?"

His eyes showed definite shock. He took a deep breath and let it out. The word *murder* usually got that reaction. But that wasn't the thing that Marlon was stuck on. Instead, he whispered, *"Four?"*

"That's right." Rylie showed him the pictures of the other girls on her phone. "Do these ring a bell? These women were found murdered, similarly to the others."

He shook his head fiercely. "I've never seen those girls in my life."

"Really?" Rylie said doubtfully. "We have a lot of evidence that says you're our man."

"Bullshit!" he cried, trying to jump up, but Michael easily shoved him in the chest, making him totter back to the sofa. "I didn't! When—what happened to those girls?"

"Just a couple of days ago. They were found smothered, and—"

"Smothered? See! I told you that's bullshit! I strangled the other girls!" he blurted smugly, his eyes widening only a second later, as the full weight of his words settled on him. "I mean . . ."

"So you did strangle Lydia Hook and Carrie Summerfield, then?" Rylie said, exchanging a glance with Michael.

His head swung side to side in denial. "No, no. What I meant was that—"

Michael sat down on the sofa next to him. "Tell us what happened. You followed them home, maybe? Thought they might be interested in you but they turned you down?"

He threw himself forward, burying his face in his hands. "Right. Look. I didn't want no trouble. They came on to me. So I thought all they needed was a little more convincing. They bought alcohol so I had to check their IDs. I found out where they lived. I stopped by their place after work. And they gave me shit. So . . .the first one, Lydia, she was a real bitch. Telling me she'd call the cops and stuff. The second one . . . she was sweet. I felt real bad about it. Told myself I'd never do it again. And I never have. That's the God's honest truth."

Michael looked over at Rylie and knew exactly what she was thinking. *If he didn't kill Marie Bottoms and Jessie Vega, then who did?*

Maybe they'd solved a cold case, which was a good thing, but Michael doubted it, too. He might have been a night janitor close to the gas station, but the method of murder was all wrong, and he'd definitely seemed confused when he saw the newest girls.

She sighed and said, "I'll go out and get the police here."

He picked up the bow, lying on the ground, and turned to their suspect. "Marlon, buddy. You're going to go to jail for a long time. You know that, right? And not just for this little stunt you played." He held up the bow.

Marlon nodded sadly. "You know what, good. I haven't been able to sleep in a year. Can't get the look on that girl's face out of my head. Maybe now, I'll finally have some peace."

Michael watched him put his head back on the sofa and close his eyes. Yes, he looked perfectly at peace. Which meant his partner *wouldn't* be. Because if what this guy was saying was true, the killer was still out there, and they needed to find a new thread to pull.

CHAPTER SEVENTEEN

Police arrived to apprehend Marlon Greef. After they'd gone over the details with the local authorities, Rylie stomped toward Michael's truck, sighing in defeat. It was coming upon noon, now, and this case that she'd hoped to find a quick end to was now likely to drag on. They'd taken one step forward, and two steps back.

"Okay, okay," Michael said as he started the engine. "Maybe it's not wrapped up in a nice, tidy bow. But we did find out who killed those girls. That's a good thing."

"I guess. Sure. You're right. It is good," she admitted.

Still, it didn't feel like enough.

"And maybe the police will question him further and find out he's our man."

She shook her head adamantly. "He's *not* our man, Bris."

Brisbane had been backing out toward the main road, but now, he stopped and looked at her. "What do you mean? Yeah, I'll admit it's iffy. But he could be lying about not killing Marie and Jessie."

"He's not," she said simply.

A crease appeared on his forehead. "And how do you figure that?"

She reached into her bag and pulled out her phone. "Because based on the crime scene photos, the killer of Jessie Vega and Marie Bottoms was right handed. And Marlon Greef was clearly left-handed. I could tell by the bow."

Michael's mouth opened, and for a moment, he didn't say anything. "Wait, how do you know the recent victims were murdered by a right-handed person?"

"Well, I don't know for sure. The killer might be ambidextrous. Because there were pressure marks on both women's shoulders from where he held them down with his left hand. Of course, he'd probably use his dominant hand to hold the pillow over her mouth. Right?"

She thrust the photo under his nose and he nodded. "Okay. I didn't notice that. Marlon could be ambidextrous, too, you know."

"No. Not likely. Left-handed bows cost a hell of a lot more. Why would anyone pay that much extra for no reason?"

He nodded. "Makes sense. Spoken like a true southpaw."

She held up her left hand and smiled. "That's right. We always get scammed, having to pay more for everything. It's discrimination."

"Hmm. I didn't realize the trauma you left-handers had to go through," he said, shifting into gear and driving onto the road. "How did you know about the bows, anyway?"

"I have a friend," she thought, thinking of her buddy Hal Buxton, her surrogate father, and how he'd bought Rylie her first bow, when she was only twelve. They'd go out hunting sometimes, and over the course of a few years, though he'd been a curmudgeonly widower and loner at first, he'd come to enjoy her company as much as she enjoyed his.

"That's mysterious. That Rich guy?"

"No. That Hal guy. Remember him?"

He nodded slowly, and said, "Right," in a way that made her think he was suspicious of her answer.

She stared at him. He'd been acting slightly jealous, ever since he'd met Cooper Rich, her old friend from the Seattle FBI office. At first, she'd insisted there was nothing going on, but then Cooper had gone and professed how much he'd missed her. Since then, he'd gone back to Seattle, but he texted her often, to check in.

But that was all. It was nothing to be jealous over.

Besides, Michael Brisbane was her partner. He had no right to be jealous about anything she did in her personal life.

"What?" she finally said.

He shrugged. "Oh, nothing. Just thought it was interesting that you know that much about archery."

"Not really. I did grow up in Wyoming. That's like, what we do."

He was about to reply when his phone rang, the call showing up on the screen on the dashboard. It was Kit.

"Wow, news travels fast. She probably wants to congratulate us for our latest victory," he remarked, pressing a button. "Yep. Hi, Kit."

"Hi, Bris. Is Rylie there with you?"

"Yeah, we're listening. You heard about Marlon Greef already, huh?"

A pause. "Bris, what in the world are you talking about?" She didn't wait for a response. "I'm calling because I just got word that there's been another murder, and it sounds pretty similar to the other ones you've been investigating."

Rylie stiffened. "Where?"

"This one's in a place called Norvander. Vera Langley, twenty-two. She was found by her boyfriend early this morning."

Rylie looked at Michael. It certainly sounded like their guy. "I saw a sign for Norvander. It's east on I-86."

"We're on our way," Michael said, surging on the gas, going almost the speed limit this time.

*

They arrived at the upscale apartment complex in the small town of Norvander shortly after noon. Michael whistled as they made their way past the police cruisers and down a cobblestone path, to the end-unit apartment. It was modern, and looked brand new. In fact, there was a mound of dirt in the field next door, where workers were pouring concrete for another foundation.

"This place is nice," Michael remarked as they walked past the manicured bushes. "Kit said the victim was only twenty-two?"

"That's right," Rylie said as they went to the front door, which was partly ajar. There was a welcome mat there and a large, wooden plaque propped up next to it that said, *SPEAK FRIEND AND ENTER.* "What does that mean?"

"Haven't you ever seen *Lord of the Rings?*" Michael asked, pushing the door open all the way and stepping inside. He called, "Anyone home?"

A police officer came toward them, a grave look on his face. "Are you the FBI agents?"

Rylie produced her credentials and made the introductions. His name was Officer Jones, and he was the senior-most official in their small police department, comprised of only three people. He'd been on the force for twenty-five years and seemed shell-shocked by this latest crime. "We've never had nothing like this, I'll tell you," he said, running his hands through salt-and-pepper curls. "They said this might be connected to those other murders I read about?"

"That's what we'll have to see," Rylie said, moving into a bright, two-story foyer with a large, dangling pendant chandelier. A couple of EMTs were standing by with a stretcher, and another man in a suit was there, as well. "So the body has not been moved yet?"

He shook his head. "When we heard you were on your way, I told them to leave everything as it is. But the coroner's been here and gotten everything he needed."

"Great," she said, motioning him forward. "That will be helpful. Could you show us?"

"Right this way."

He led them down a long corridor with plush carpet. Rylie could see the victim, lying, face up, on the floor, just outside one of the bedrooms. Her arms and legs were bare and her blonde hair was splayed out. There was a small accent pillow beside her face.

As Rylie crouched in front of the body, she said, "Were pictures taken?"

He nodded.

She moved the pillow aside and checked for any other signs of struggle. She pushed aside the victim's shirt and saw bruising, similar to that of the other victims, indicating that the killer had pushed his weight into her chest. Her fingernails were also curled, which indicated that she might have put up a fight. "We'll want to have them scrape underneath her fingernails, for any DNA."

"Already done," the officer said, looking sadly down at the woman.

Michael looked around. "Was there a sign of forced entry?"

"Nope. We think the killer came in through the open window in the living room."

The officer said, "So, what are we thinking? Is it the same guy you're looking for?"

It certainly seemed like it. But then again, they'd just learned of two murders they thought were related to it that were not. So she didn't answer with a definite. "It looks like it. But we don't have any DNA evidence on the last two. Let's hope this one finally gives us some. Who found the body?"

"A young man. Her boyfriend," the officer said, motioning them to follow him. "He'd called and texted her and got no response, which was unlike her, so he came to check on her. He's a little torn up, so I told him to wait outside and take a breather."

The officer led them out through a vast, two-story living room, part of which was full of boxes. Rylie paused, looking in one of them. "So she didn't live with him? Did she just move in?"

The officer nodded and pulled back a sliding glass door to a small patio, enclosed on all sides by a high, fiberglass fence. A man with a beard, jeans, and work boots was sitting on the steps, smoking a cigarette.

He jumped up and threw it down, stubbing it out as they came out.

Officer Jones said, "George Bingham, meet FBI agents Rylie Wolf and Michael Brisbane. They want to ask you some questions."

"Uh, sure," he said nervously, shaking their hands. "Anything I can do. I just . . . am a little rattled right now. I can't believe anyone would do this."

"Yeah, I can imagine it's a shock," Michael said, motioning to the step as Officer Jones retreated inside. "Would you say you're the person who's closest to her?"

Rylie expected a quick yes, but he hesitated. "I don't know. I—I wanted to be. She has a lot of friends, too."

The man was fidgeting from foot to foot, like a little kid that had to use the bathroom. It unnerved Rylie, and obviously did the same to Michael because he said, "Sit. We won't take long. You can get us a list of her friends?"

He stroked his beard and nodded. "Yeah, anything I can do. And I got nowhere to be, so ask me anything. I called out from work. I can't go in . . . not like this."

"Where do you work, Mr. Bingham?" Rylie asked.

His stroking of his beard became a double-handed effort, as he started dragging his hands down his cheeks to his chin. His eyes were glassy and red. "I work at Tony's Farm Supply. I'm an associate there."

"And what did Vera do?"

"She worked for TAYS-T, the pet food supply company. She was a junior manager of procurement there. Really smart. She was going places. That's where she was last night. She had a conference in Pierre. For people who wanted to be managers. She was ambitious. She was . . ." he paused, trying to find the words, and his voice cracked. "I was really proud of her. I didn't know what she saw in a loser like me."

"When was the last time you spoke to her?"

He sniffed loudly and wiped his nose with his flannel shirtsleeve. "Well, let's see. It was last night. I wasn't sure when she was coming back. Thought we could go out after. But she said she was going to be coming back late, and that she'd talk to me tomorrow. Which was today."

"Did you try to get in touch with her after that?"

He nodded. "I called her a bunch of times. Texted, too. Nothing. So I just wanted to check on her. It's like I told the police, I got here around seven, let myself in, and found her . . .lying just like that. You saw, right?"

"You had a key to the apartment?" Rylie asked.

"Yeah. She gave me one." His lips twisted, his eyes faraway, caught in some memory. "She was pretty set on the fact that we didn't live together, though. Waiting for us to be married, she said. I was going to pop the question when I had enough to buy a ring."

"And though you were worried about her last night, you waited until the morning to drive here? Where were you last night?"

He looked up at her, his brow furrowing. "I was out shooting pool with my buddies at the bar near where I live. Other side of town. I got pretty wasted, I guess, 'cause last thing I remember was texting her to see if she'd gotten home yet. Then I woke up in my bed. No way could I have driven there. My boys must've brought me home."

Rylie looked around the patio. It was spotless and empty. "She just moved in here, hmm?"

"Not *just*. She's been here a few months. But she never got around to doing much to the place. Always working. I told her if she let me move in, I'd help her fix it up. She didn't want that," he said, his hands now moving to his eyes, rubbing them. "If I'd have been here, things would've been different. If only she hadn't been so damn stubborn!"

He smacked both of his thighs with his hands and his body seemed to deflate like a balloon.

"That was the way she was. Stubborn," he said, almost to himself.

"So you don't know if she stopped anywhere on the way home from Pierre?" Michael asked. "Like a gas station or something?"

He shook his head. "She wouldn't have."

Rylie thought that was a good question, considering the other victims had stopped at the Gas-o-Rama, and it was on her route. His denial deflated her. "Why not?"

"She didn't like filling up her own tank. She didn't like the smell of gas, or getting it on her hands. I always did that for her. Besides, her tank was almost full. Filled it up for her the day before."

"But she might have stopped for a drink or something? Maybe to use the restroom?" Michael pressed.

"Doubtful."

93

"And why's that?" Rylie asked, getting a bit annoyed. Right now, that gas station was their best connection between the two victims. If they didn't have that, what did they have?

"Because she didn't like stopping at places like that," he said with a shrug. "It skeeved her out."

"But a new place, if she really had to go . . ." Rylie said. "Maybe she'd make an exception?"

"Nah. Not on her life. If she really had to go to the bathroom, she'd hold it until she exploded, I suspect." He paused, then reached for a cigarette in his breast pocket, twirling it between his fingers. "You see, she'd had something happen to her when she was in high school. I know because we've known each other since we were kids. She was at a gas station with her friends and a guy came in and waved a gun around. She was always really antsy about stuff like that, since. So I know she'd go to the conference, and come right back."

Rylie gnawed on the inside of her cheek. That was great. They'd looked into Vera's credit cards, and they revealed no other charges. So she didn't stop *anywhere*. That blew apart the thought process Rylie had been having up until now. She felt like, based on the previous routes of the girls, they'd all stopped off on an exit somewhere, met up with the same person, who had checked their IDs, just like Marlon had checked IDs, to find out where they lived. Well, not in the case of Jessie Vega. Maybe he'd just followed her to the hotel. But somewhere, they'd stopped, and the killer had targeted them.

But if Vera Langley hadn't stopped anywhere, then where could she have met her killer?

"Are you sure?" she asked, her voice sounding weak, desperate.

"Yeah. Definitely. Only thing is . . ."

"Yes?" Michael prompted.

"Well, it's nothing, really, and I'm not one to speak ill of the dead," he said, looking at the ground. "But when she started this new job, I got the feeling that she met another guy. She started acting all uppity. Stuck up, a little. Like she wasn't one of us, if you know what I mean? That's why she moved into this place, even though I wasn't sure she could afford it. It was like, someone there made her change. I kept asking if she had another guy. And then . . ."

"Go on," Rylie said.

He shook his head. "It's stupid. But she went to this conference with the owner of TAYS-T. He's an old guy. She said he was really

94

kind, taking her under his wing, teaching her the ropes. But I don't know. She said she wouldn't be home from the conference until late. But I looked it up online. The conference ended, mid-day. So yeah . . . I don't know what she was up to. That's the reason I came by looking for her. I was kind of thinking she'd found someone else."

Rylie's eyes met with Michael's, who nodded. That was something. Another lead. "You said the name of the place was Tasty?"

"Yeah. Uh, T-A-Y-S-T. It's the big white factory building you probably saw when you came into town. He owns it. His name is . . ." He paused, thinking. "Ed. Ed something. I can't remember. She talked about him all the time—how great he was, how wonderful— but I kind of tuned it out." He laughed bitterly.

"Thanks, George," Michael said, patting his shoulder. "You've been a big help. I'm real sorry for your loss."

George nodded but said nothing as they left the patio.

As they walked through the apartment, Rylie scanned it. It was definitely impersonal, with white, unadorned walls and hardly any furniture. Poor Vera had obviously been far too busy to enjoy her fancy new living space.

"So, what do you say?" Michael asked, fishing his keys out of his pockets as they walked toward the parking lot. "Should we go to this pet food place and talk to this guy Ed, her boss?"

Rylie nodded. "I think we have to. If what George said is true, he's the last person who saw her alive."

CHAPTER EIGHTEEN

"Isn't that the cutest thing you've ever seen?"

Rylie looked up from the TAYS-T website to find Michael, beaming at the logo for TAYS-T pet food. It was a picture of a giant, floppy-eared dog, tongue out, over the letters TAYS-T.

She wrinkled her nose. "I don't really like dogs," she murmured, pointing at the screen. "The owner's name is Ed Barnes. And he doesn't just look old enough to be her father. He looks old enough to be her *grandfather*."

He let out a laugh, then looked over at her. "Jeez. Hell. Now I really think something's wrong with you. First cats, now man's best friend?"

She shrugged. "I don't know. I've never actually had a pet."

"That's a mistake," he muttered, shaking his head. "Not even a goldfish? Damn. I had a Golden Retriever growing up. Dougie. That was his name. I still miss him. First thing I'm gonna do when I settle down is—"

He'd stopped the car, so she opened up the door before he could take her any further down memory lane. Sometimes his stories were so long, they never had an end. She sensed this was one of them.

As they walked in front of the big, white metal-sided warehouse, they passed a lot more of the logo with the puppy on it. It was everywhere—on the signs, the benches outside, the doors to the lobby. Every time Michael looked at it, he smiled.

She had to laugh. *Sometimes he's so amused by the simplest of things.*

In the lobby, it smelled like pet food, pungent yet not entirely terrible. There were pet foods displays among the potted plants and red vinyl-covered chairs, and a number of brochures advertising their different food products. Michael picked one up and began to read it as Rylie went to the sliding glass window at reception.

An older woman with a tight perm slid the window open. "Hi, what can I do for you?"

"Yes, we'd like to speak to your owner . . . Ed Barnes?"

"Do you have an appointment?"

She shook her head.

"Well, Mr. Barnes is very busy, but what is this in reference to?"

Rylie produced her credentials, and the woman's tone changed immediately.

"Oh. Of course." She reached for her phone and slid the window closed. Though Rylie couldn't hear her, the woman kept glancing up at her as she spoke. Finally, she set the receiver down, slid the window open, and said, "Mr. Barnes will be right out to see you."

"Thank you," Rylie said, meandering around the large, empty lobby. She wasn't interested in pet food, but her eyes caught on a framed photograph, over a line of chairs. It was a picture of a number of people, posing together. A plaque underneath said, *BEST PLACE TO WORK IN SOUTH DAKOTA- TAYS-T*

She scanned the smiling faces of the employees and noticed Vera at once—the youngest, prettiest one, and the only blonde. She was standing toward the middle of the group, next to an inordinately tan man with a head full of shockingly white hair. He had his arm around her. Rylie knew him from the website. It was Ed Barnes, the owner.

Just then, the door opened behind her, and she faced Ed Barnes in the flesh.

He seemed a little less tan, a little frailer. But it was definitely him. "FBI?" he said, equal parts curiosity and kindness, stretching out his hand for a shake. "That's a little surprising. What is this in regards to?"

Rylie shook his hand. "Yes, I'm Special Agent Rylie Wolf. This is Michael Brisbane. Can we speak somewhere in private?"

"Sure," he said, his tone becoming serious for a moment, before he let out a laugh. "I'm not in trouble, am I?"

Michael glanced at the receptionist, who was eyeing them curiously. "No. Let's go find a quiet place to talk?"

"Right. Of course." The man turned on his heel and brought them inside, onto a large manufacturing floor. Uniformed people walked around in goggles and hairnets, and the buzz of machinery filled the air. He spoke over the din. "This is my little operation. Well, it's not so little anymore. I started out selling this stuff out of my house. And now, in our fiftieth year, we're international. We have outfits in France and China, believe it or not."

"That's great," Michael said, as a couple of dogs began to bark from the other side of the floor. Suddenly, they rushed at them.

97

"Here come my puppies!" Ed Barnes said, grinning like proud papa.

Michael put out his hands to welcome them with open arms. Rylie took a step away. Of course, both of them attacked Rylie first. She put her hands up, grimacing, as the dogs nosed at her thighs. "Uh . . . what are they doing?" she whispered to him.

"Wow. You really do not like dogs. How is that even possible?"

She gritted her teeth. "Why are they looking at me like that?"

"Hmm. They want you to pet them, maybe?" He said it like the answer was obvious.

Slowly, carefully, she put her hand down and stroked the fur between their ears. That wasn't so bad. In fact, they were kind of cute. But she didn't like the fact that both men were looking at her like she was insane, and she hated being off her game. Yes, she understood it—she was probably the only person who'd ever grown up without a pet, but Rick Wolf had been too neat, and Hal's wife had been the same way. And after that, in college, at Quantico, and then in Seattle, there just hadn't been time. "Nice," she said, "But please, let's continue."

She followed Ed into a small conference room with executive leather chairs, all situated around a modern oak desk. As she sat down, she was startled to realize the two dogs, German Shepherds? Retrievers?—she wasn't sure—had followed her and were now sniffing at her, wanting more pets.

"They like you," Michael observed.

She noticed that. He seemed jealous again, but mostly because *he'd* wanted their attention, and they hadn't even looked at him. "They have good taste," she mumbled, wanting to get this started. "Mr. Barnes."

He closed the door and sat down at the head of the table. "What can I do for you?"

"You have an employee, Vera Langley, correct?"

He nodded, his brow wrinkling. "Is something wrong?"

"It's after noon," Rylie said. "You weren't concerned about her not showing up?"

"No, of course not," he said, and paused, collecting his thoughts. "We went to a conference and dinner, and I sent her home late last night. So I told her she could come in today, as late as she wanted. Is something wrong?"

Michael leaned forward, lacing his hands in front of him. "Yes, unfortunately. I'm sorry to say that Vera is dead."

"Dead?" The old man repeated the word, almost to himself. "Oh, no. Was it a car accident?"

"No," Rylie said, her tone grave. "She was murdered in her home."

He put a hand to his mouth, and he seemed to tremble a bit. "Oh, my God. This is horrible. How . . . do you know who did it?"

"No, but we were hoping you could help us try to reconstruct her last moments, since we believe you might be the last person who saw her alive. You were with her last night?"

He nodded. "I was with her until about ten or eleven. We went to a restaurant in Pierre after the conference, and had a long talk about her future with the company," he said his voice hollow. "Vera . . . she was young, but she was very good at what she did. I really thought that she might take over for me one day, when I retired."

Rylie frowned, George's words coming to her. *I was kind of thinking she'd found someone else.* Was Ed the person she'd found? Yes, she was young, but ambitious, and stranger things had happened. He didn't seem too much like a creeper, but one never could tell. "Did you two have a relationship?"

His eyes went wide. "Purely a professional one, I assure you. She had a young boyfriend. But I got the feeling she was on the fence about him. Whenever she talked of him, it wasn't in a positive light. Once, she said he was lazy. I think he might have been holding her back. And I was looking for someone to handle my international accounts, which meant a lot of travel. She didn't bat an eyelash at that."

"Did she say she was going to stop anywhere on her way home?"

"No. In fact, it was so late, she said she just wanted to get to bed. That's when I told her she didn't have to come in right away today." He pressed his lips together, staring out into space. "I just . . . it's incredible. She was such a sweet girl. I don't think she had any enemies. If anything . . . I'd look into that boyfriend of hers. Maybe he confronted her, and she told him she didn't want to be with him. Maybe he just snapped."

Rylie sighed. George's alibi, playing pool with his friends, could be easily verified, and besides, he just hadn't given off that impression. He'd been devastated, not nervous or squirrely. She said, "So she never mentioned that she needed gas, or that she was going to stop anywhere?"

"No . . ." he murmured, but suddenly, he pounded his fist on the conference table and shook a finger at them. "Wait. I just thought of

99

something. There was a guy. He used to work in the back warehouse of my outfit, loading the trucks. John Fielding."

"What about him?" Michael said.

"He was a creep. I had to fire him. He was constantly going after the girls. Stalking them, following them home, trying his luck with them," he said, shaking his head. "You ask any of the women here, they'd tell you. He wasn't sane."

"You let him go?"

"Oh, yeah, of course. He made a big stink about it, too, went out of this place like a tornado, throwing things, cursing his head off. Real loose cannon. I thought I was going to have to call the police to get him to leave. And after he left, I had them lock the door, in case he came back with a pistol."

Michael whistled. "Sounds unstable, to say the least."

"Yeah, tell me about it. I interview all the people who come to work for me, myself. I couldn't believe I made such a mistake. The weasel gave me fake references, fake employment history, and I just went with it. Turned out to be all phony. He'd been in jail a couple times. For assaulting females, theft, you name it. Never felt so bad."

Rylie made a mental note of the name. "And do you think this John Fielding might've had contact with Vera?"

"Yeah, definitely. I fired him only a couple months ago. She'd been working for me a while by then. And part of her job was to go from department to department, checking things out. So yeah. I'm pretty sure they interacted." He drummed his fingers on the table. "I can get you the info he provided me, but like I said, I don't know if it's accurate."

"That's all right. If he has a record, we'll be able to find him," Rylie said, standing up. As she did, the dogs followed her. She gave them pets. "Thanks for the information. And we're sorry about the bad news."

When they reached Michael's car, she got on her phone, already asking Beaker to provide John Fielding's arrest record. He sent it almost instantly, so by the time she climbed in the truck, she was deeply embroiled in his sordid history. "His rap sheet is a mile long," she said, scrolling. "No murder, though."

"And is there any connection to the other victims?"

"Maybe there is. But he just got out of jail for drugs a week ago. Maybe he's escalating."

"Could be," Michael said, starting up his truck. "Does it give you an address there?"

"Yeah. Well, as part of his probation, he's working for a construction company. I'll call them and find out where he's been working."

Based on what Ed had said, she knew this interview with John Fielding would be no picnic. But if he brought them closer to finding out what had happened to these women, it would be worth it.

CHAPTER NINETEEN

Rylie tapped her fingers on the passenger-side armrest of Michael's truck as he sped toward the construction site where John Fielding had been dispatched. According to the administrative assistant at the J B Bower Construction Co., where he'd been working ever since he got out on probation two months ago, he had completed training as a bricklayer while in prison.

The day had been getting warmer and warmer, and now it was far hotter than any day she'd ever experienced since moving out to South Dakota. She shrugged off her jacket and cracked a window.

"Let's just hope this guy's in a good mood," she said, turning the vents so the air hit her face. "It's really hot. Working outside in this heat, I don't know how anyone could be."

Michael shrugged. "Something tells me that's wishful thinking. Just seeing us is going to piss him off."

That was the truth. Even when a person with a rap sheet had done no wrong, they automatically tensed up when the FBI came around. It was like they were just waiting for the cuffs to be snapped on them.

As the administrative assistant had explained to them, John Fielding was now working at the site of a new upscale retirement community, pretty much out in the middle of nowhere. They'd driven for miles through field after field, only to finally come to a giant billboard that said, *SWIFT MEADOW—LUXURY HOMESITES FOR 55+, NOW BUILDING! ONE MILE STRAIGHT AHEAD!*

At that, Michael actually pressed on the gas and went faster than the fifty-mile-per-hour speed limit. He must've been excited, too.

The map of the homesites on the billboard had showed line after line of perfect little brick houses, but the site itself showed nothing of the sort. In fact, it was mostly piles of dirt, stretching for miles, surrounded by a cornfield. There was a single unpaved road leading up to a trailer, a few trucks parked in front, and six homes, all in varying stages of completion.

They had just stepped onto the dirt road leading to the office when they noticed a man, standing in front of the façade of one of the houses and staring at them. He was wearing a yellow construction cap, dirty jeans, and a white t-shirt, and stripping off his gloves.

"Now, that looks like he could be our man," Michael said. "What do you think?"

Rylie nodded. "Let's go."

They'd barely taken a single step toward the man when he threw his gloves down and took off, racing around the side of the building.

"No!" Rylie shouted, breaking into a run. She felt Michael behind her and called, "Go around the other side of the house!"

He'd already been heading that way. "On it," he huffed, and raced up a dirt-covered incline, barely breaking stride when he hit the top of it and lunged over a narrow gully.

The mud was thick, but that did nothing to slow her. In fact, as the trees bordering the dirt road thickened and seemed to envelop her, she pushed on faster. The adrenaline coursing through her veins seemed to release an energy in her that she only felt at times like these. It seemed alive, exhilarating. It was not out of fear, but more like a need, a want. Maybe even a temptation. She wasn't sure, but she could feel those answers she so desperately sought were out there, close. She wanted to get to the bottom of it, and quickly.

Slowing as she reached the edge of the house and realizing he was nowhere in sight, she took in her surroundings. There was nothing beyond this area but a tall cornfield. Had he gone in there?

Michael appeared at the back edge of the house at the same time she did, scanning the area. "Where'd he go?"

She lifted a finger to her lips, willing her heart to stop beating so she could listen. She heard it very faintly—the sound of something, rustling through the cornfield ahead.

She quickened her step again, a stream of sweat rolling down her back as the wind braced her, whipping her ponytail across her cheek. She instinctively pulled at her shirt as she crunched over the dead leaves beneath her feet. She looked over her shoulder periodically to make sure Michael was still following close behind. With his long strides, he was doing a good job keeping up with her, even though she was in better shape. But his right hand was already hovering over his sidearm. He was nervous, too. She didn't blame him though; they already knew what this man was capable of.

But the deeper they got into the cornfield—the more certain Rylie became that guns were not going to be much help to them.

Rylie's heart pounded again, and her lungs were begging for a break when she came to the edge of the field, and another dirt road. Beyond that, more corn. There was a small iron barricade blocking the road, there to keep trespassing cars out.

"Hold up." Michael panted, resting his hands on his knees. "What is our plan?"

"I don't know. I don't know where he went. He must still be in the field. Let's move."

They paused for only a moment longer before stepping carefully around the iron bar. As they moved forward, Rylie glanced back over her shoulder. She once again felt like someone was following, watching them. But the only thing she saw behind them was the stalks of corn, swaying in the breeze.

When they cleared the dirt road, they made a straight line for the second field. As they neared the rows, Rylie gave a hand signal, indicating that she would take the rows on the right and he would run down further to take the rows on the left.

Michael gave a nod and kept running to the far end of the field, about a quarter of a mile farther down. Meanwhile, she ducked into the cornfield and walked along the nearest row. She knew the rustling of stalks and leaves would give away any hope of sneaking up on the man, but that was fine. Still, she walked as quietly as she could so she could hear any commotion ahead of her. She kept her gun in her holster, but the deeper she went into the field, the more unsure she was, and the harder it became to fight the urge to pull it out.

At a place she assumed to be somewhere near the center, she stopped, looked around, and cut over several rows. and stopped when she heard movement nearby. She took off again, leaping across rows and trying to make as little noise as possible.

There it was again. Unmistakable. Footsteps. Someone was moving through the corn. The stalks were swaying gently, dead husks crunching underfoot. Rylie moved through the corn, jumping another row, where she saw a figure moving, limping towards the front of the field. It was hunched over as if in tremendous pain, staggering aimlessly through the rows.

Rylie drew closer, her eyes wide, hands shaking slightly as she pulled her firearm from her holster.

"Stop!" She shouted. "FBI!"

The figure turned slowly. It was John Fielding. And from what Rylie could tell, he was alone.

He didn't stop long enough for her to aim her gun. His eyes darted to the side. Before she could say another word, he dodged between the rows of corn.

"Michael!" she shouted. "He's here!"

Rylie took off in the direction of the other end of the cornfield, acting on gut instinct. She'd known the moment she heard about this man where it was going to lead them— it wouldn't be easy. And now, she was nearly out of breath, with insects buzzing around her sweat-soaked skin. Slapping away low hanging corn leaves and husks, Rylie barreled towards the end of the cornfield, unsure of her direction. Was she heading back toward the houses? All she could see in every direction was corn, framed by a cloudless blue sky.

But she didn't want to stay in one place. Inaction wasn't her thing. So she paused, listened for the sound of footsteps, and then took off in that direction.

As she ran through the stalks, she hit another gear, wondering if Michael had come out the other end yet and, if so, if he had found anything. "Michael!"

It took another three minutes of flat-out running, zigzagging between the rows as insects buzzed in her ears, but Rylie finally came to the end of the cornfield. It *was* the end, someplace she'd never been before, far away from the new homes under construction. She found herself staring at the thin strip of tall grass that separated the property from the forests behind it.

She looked to the right, but only saw the cornfield, stretching on, well out of her sight. If Michael was already out, she'd have to walk a pretty good distance to find him. She could—

Her focus on the little stretch of field was broken by the sound of something moving through the forest ahead. Pounding footsteps.

She did not hesitate. *It could be anything,* she thought as she took off towards the trees, readjusting her grip on her gun as she went. *An animal. Or . . .*

Her legs were already screaming at her from the steady jog through the corn, but she pushed past it. She listened for any human sound as she made her way past the tree line, but there was nothing. In fact, aside from her footfalls, the woods were eerily quiet. It reminded her of the still sort of heaviness to the atmosphere in the moments before a loud summer thunderstorm.

She carried on into the woods, coming to the gradual downward grade to the land that led to a small, squat storage shed, broken and decaying from rust. As she carefully made her way down, she noticed a figure, just beyond the trees. At first, she thought it was an animal. But as she got closer, she realized it was Michael. He was lying on the ground.

Gasping, Rylie ran forward, and realizing she too could be in danger, stopped short. She lifted her gun, scanning the area.

She slowly turned, Glock in one hand, and she searched the area. She heard Michael's faint moaning and made it over to him, finding him lying on his side, gasping for air.

Rylie knelt by his side and saw a trickle of blood by his temple. "Michael? Are you . . .?"

He wiped at the side of his head and rolled over, his eyes opening. "Rylie?" he asked, blinking hard.

"Yeah, it's me," she said nervously, looking around. "What happened? We've got to—"

Before she could finish, something she couldn't see collided with her from behind, knocking the wind out of her and throwing her forward. She lost hold of her gun as she struck the ground.

She quickly got to her knees, fumbling for her Glock. Vision swimming, she fanned her hands out and grabbed ahold of the butt of the gun, spinning, and aiming at once. She caught sight of their target right as he was about to dodge between the trees.

"John Fielding! FBI! Stop, or I swear, I'll shoot!"

He had no intention of stopping. Not pausing, not looking back, he rushed up the incline, the steepness of it making him stumble. He reached out and grabbed a tree branch to steady himself, then grabbed it, tearing it free.

She aimed. "Freeze!"

He didn't. He swung at her. She ducked and fired off a shot, hitting the small tree, making it tremble. He winced, dropped the branch, and put his hands over his head as a shield. Without the support, he started to slide back on the loose gravel. Catching himself in the slide, he froze.

"All right, all right," he called, making the effort to turn on the steep embankment. "I'm not running. You got me."

Michael was sitting up, wiping the blood from his temple. "Scumbag clocked me with a branch."

Rylie rushed to the man, grabbed the cuffs from her belt, and snapped them onto his fleshy wrists. She shoved him down to the ground so he was sitting. "What were you running from?"

"I dunno. You looked like detectives," he mumbled, lifting both hands to wipe the sweat from his brow. "I thought you were after me for something I done. Every time one of you comes for me, it's always trouble."

Michael shook his head and pulled out a plastic bag filled with what looked like white powder. "I caught him trying to ditch this stuff."

Still pointing the gun at him, she went over and looked at the crumpled bag. "Heroin?"

Michael nodded. "That's my guess."

The man shook his head sadly. "I'm just holding them for a friend," he said, so tonelessly it was as if he didn't believe the excuse, either.

"Right. We've heard it before," Michael snapped, standing up and dusting the pine needles and dried grass from his dark slacks. "What I want to know is, where were you last night?"

His eyes narrowed. "Last night? What do you. . ."

Rylie, exhausted from the run, let out an exasperated sigh. "Just answer the question."

"I was working. I finished up here at around eight and then I went to a bar to play some pool and blow off some steam. Why?"

"Do you know a Vera Langley?"

He stared blankly. "Who?"

"You worked at a place called TAYS-T pet food, right?" Rylie asked.

"Yeah . . ." His face lit up. "Oh, right. That blonde girl who wore the tight skirts. What about her?"

"Did you see her last night?"

He shook his head. "I wish. I was alone at the bar. There were slim pickings there, I tell you. I drank myself into a stupor and then I went home." His smile faded. "Wait. Why you asking me this? Is she . . . did something happen to her? I didn't do nothing. Who gave you my name? I swear, I haven't seen her since I was let go. That's the truth."

"All right. The name of the bar you went to?" Michael asked. "Anyone who can verify your story?"

"Smith's. On Elm Street. You can speak to Bob. He's the owner and the bartender. Served me all my drinks."

The agents looked at each other and Rylie shook her head. He wasn't their man. Then who was?

As Michael pulled him up to standing, John said, "She's dead, huh? Always knew that girl was going to get it. She was ambitious, you know? Sticking her nose where it didn't belong all the time. Women need to shut up and know their place, am I right?"

He scowled at Rylie.

"All right, all right," Michael muttered, shoving him up the incline. "Shut up and come with me."

"Wait. What's going to happen to me?" he said, his body suddenly tensing. "You ain't gonna—"

"Oh yes, we are," Rylie said, proud to be able to inform him of this. "It's our duty to tell the parole board about your little probation violation here."

His scowl deepened. "I ain't done nothing wrong!"

They ignored him for the rest of the walk, back through the cornfields, and toward the homesites. There, Rylie called for the police to come and pick him up, and as they waited for the police to arrive, they spread a map out over the hood of Michael's truck, trying to decide where to go next. Rylie marked each of the three murders on the map, hoping that seeing it laid out would provide a pattern, giving them intel on where to go next.

But it was just a giant triangle, with I-86 going straight down the center. An area over a hundred miles wide, and just as long. The killer could strike anywhere inside or outside of that.

Her shoulders sagged in her defeat. She looked over at Michael, whose temple, right near his eye, was swelling an angry purple. The bleeding had slowed, but Michael's eye was swelling shut, and either he was wincing, or the injury was making him look that way. "Are you going to be all right?"

"Yeah," he said gruffly.

"No, let me have a look," she said, coming up close to him and gingerly touching the injury. "You should probably get checked—"

"No," he said, skirting away from her. "Forget it."

"I think you should," she said, trapping him between herself and the hood of his truck, getting in his face, all but forcing him to let her take a better look. "You might have—"

He nudged her off, not making eye contact. "I said, I'm *fine*."

The forcefulness of his words was effective. He rarely raised his voice, so when he did this time, she listened. A moment of awkwardness passed between them, and she wasn't quite sure what it meant. *What just happened?*

It was broken when he leaned over the map. "Where do we go next, then?"

She didn't answer, at first. She really wasn't sure, and was still a little confused over his reaction when she'd tried to touch him. Was it too intimate? She'd just been trying to tend to his injury.

After a minute, she said, "I guess we should go through that list of Vera's friends that George gave us, and see if they know anything."

It felt like grasping at straws, but it was their last hope.

CHAPTER TWENTY

The man took a sip from his giant mug of coffee and tried not to inhale the smelly fumes from the giant dump truck, screaming away from his station and leaving a black, caustic cloud in its wake.

When he was younger, things like that had bothered him. Sounds. Smells. Not anymore.

At first, he'd thought he'd go mad at a job like this. After his first day, three months ago, he was certain he'd never make it a full week. Standing on one's feet for eight hours at a time, taking sweaty money from annoying strangers, making change, smiling, and saying "have a nice day" time after time after time? He thought he'd never be able to pull it off.

But he'd needed the money. He also knew that no one would hire a man with his history and pay quite so well.

So he stuck it out, developed a thick skin.

It helped that he'd made a game of it.

Yes, his game was fun. The only way he knew to make it through this unbearably shitty job.

"Ten minute break," Olaf, the relief guy, said behind him, sliding open the door to his booth.

Hallelujah, he thought, giving Olaf a thumb's up. His bladder was about to burst, a casualty of the coffee he chugged non-stop to stay awake during these dull hours. He headed for the door.

Olaf merely scowled at him, keeping his distance.

No one he worked with liked him, but that was fine by him. He was used to that. All through school, he'd been the "weird one." And he got it. Buck teeth, Coke-bottle glasses, egg-shaped body, a penchant for laughing too loud at the wrong times. He couldn't help it. But he didn't mind. He'd thought, eventually, he'd find his tribe.

Never did, though. That was fine, though. He'd found someone to marry him. He'd thought that was enough.

Turned out, he'd been better off alone.

110

He jogged across the center lane, toward Betty's booth, and waved at her as he passed in front of a sportscar, whose driver was handing over a dollar. She scowled back and shook her head in distaste.

Betty was older than the hills. A total bitch. But he liked to tease her, to see just how bitchy she could get.

That was another thing about him. He liked to try people's patience. It was his art, a technique he'd perfected over the years. He already knew his appearance repulsed them, so there was no point in working twice as hard to get on their good side. By being kind and polite, he found most simply forgot about him. It was much easier to make his mark by doing the opposite. He'd learned to have fun with it. To see how much he could annoy them, push them to their limits. Making people act in unexpected ways was something he took pride in.

Just like his wife, Virginia, had said. *You test my limits, Ralphie. Every day. I can't wait until you're gone. When you die, it'll be the happiest day of my life.*

He shrugged off the sour feeling he got whenever he thought of her, those piercing blue eyes, that pretty face of hers that masked such pure, unbridled evil. Even in her sickest days, her words could pack the strongest, most painful punch.

He'd learned from the best.

He jogged to the restroom in the office and relieved himself, trying not to think of her. Instead, he thought of the food in the vending machine outside. He'd get a bag of chips and some raspberry licorice sticks for the last half of his shift. Not healthy, but that was the point. His wife always made healthy, inedible stuff, and gave him flack for his growing belly.

Now, he was not just chubby. He was fat. And he didn't care.

The women had been repulsed by him, just as his wife had been. They all looked like her, with those blue eyes and a heart-shaped face. He'd enjoyed covering those faces with a pillow, stifling every last breath, until they stopped squirming beneath him.

He realized, on the way back from the vending machine, that he wanted another one.

Now.

This was the perfect shift. Tonight, he'd get off at one, and he could play. Or maybe, if the right girl came along, he'd beg off early. Say he wasn't feeling well. Olaf would let him go. They weren't friends, like some employees were with their employers, but he was the most reliable employee on the force.

He just needed to find the right girl.

As he crossed the lanes of traffic to his booth, he had to run so he didn't wind up a hood ornament on a Cadillac. He got back to his booth, Olaf spun around and left without so much as a "Have a nice day."

He slid the door shut behind him, enclosing him in the small space. His supervisors had told him that if he gained any more weight, he wouldn't be able to fit in the booth anymore. It didn't bother him. He was good at what he did. They said he was an asset. He showed up to work on time and never complained, and never called in sick.

Yes, he'd been good. He could use a little fun again, tonight.

He watched as a car came by—typical female car, a sky blue SUV with something fuzzy dangling from the rearview mirror. Maybe . . .

He rehearsed his spiel in his head as she pulled up and rolled down her window.

Disappointment flooded him as he realized it was a woman in her fifties, with dark eyes, and a ruddy, chubby face. His face fell.

Clutching coins, she waved her hand in front of him. "*Hello?*" she snapped.

Her voice was just like his ex-wife, full of contempt. But that was where the similarities ended. No, on this desolate route, this woman might wind up being his best chance. But he couldn't bring himself to. It wouldn't be right.

She dropped fifty cents in his hand. "I don't have anything else."

He just stared at the two coins in his palm, damp from having been between that woman's plump, sweaty fingers.

"Do you need to take my license or something?"

He shook his head and waved her on. It was such a disappointment, he didn't want to bother. "Have a good—"

He stopped because she'd already taken off, her window powering up. He sighed. Another car came up, and he had to make change for a twenty.

As he handed the bills back to the driver, he thought about the last one. Pretty girl, dressed well, nice home. She'd been nice to him, but he could see through that. Eventually, that would change. She was a bitch, just like all of them. Thought they were princesses, and that they could order the men in their lives around. She'd had a guy. He'd seen a picture of him on the mantle when he'd climbed in her window. Handsome, smiling, with no idea what he was in for.

In a way, he'd saved him. The man didn't realize it now, but he owed him a debt of gratitude.

It had been a tight squeeze, through that window. But she'd never heard a thing.

He smiled, thinking of how surprised she'd been when he appeared in the hallway, next to her. She'd looked just like his wife had, once.

He loved that look she'd given him. They all did the same. At that moment, they realized that *he*, finally, held all the cards. It was a look that made him feel suddenly powerful.

And he wanted to feel it again. No. He *needed* to.

The next car that pulled up was a rugged four by four. He expected a twenty-something guy with a baseball cap and saggy cargo shorts. Instead, he was pleasantly surprised by its occupant. It was a young woman with brown hair, maybe a bit darker than he'd have liked. She was wearing a rumpled blouse, exposing far more cleavage than Virginia would've. But she had the small face, the blue eyes, the pale skin.

Just like her.

"I'm sorry!" she said, her voice cracking as she dug frantically in the purse on her lap for the change. "I know I had a dollar when I left, but I can't seem to find it anywhere!"

He fought back the smile that wanted to force its way to his lips. "You don't have the money?" he asked, his voice low and stern.

"No! I don't! I can't—" She froze and looked up at him, eyes pleading. "I'm sorry. I'm not in trouble, am I?"

"Yes, it's serious. It is a felony to try to skip out on tolls."

Her eyes went wide. "Oh, God. But I didn't mean to—"

He pointed to the side of the road. "Pull over to the shoulder. I'll need to make a photocopy of your license."

"Yes. Okay." She shoved aside her purse, wrapped her slim fingers around the wheel, and navigated to the side of the road.

Her obedience was endearing, but he knew things like that did not last long. Not with these bitches. He watched her go, and this time, he allowed himself to smile. As he slid open the door to his booth and headed across the lane to take down her information, a spring came to his step.

Tonight, he would have his fun.

CHAPTER TWENTY ONE

When Rylie and Michael walked through the door of the café, two of Vera's best friends from high school, Anne and Willa, were already there, sitting in a booth. They were both young, probably only twenty-three or so, and one, Anne, had tattoos up and down her arms. Willa was almost the opposite, her hair in a ponytail, wearing a soft pink sweater and pearls. As they neared, Anne looked absolutely mortified. Willa, unfazed, was filing her nails, not making eye contact with any of them.

"Good afternoon, detectives," Willa said, her mouth a thin line as they took their seats.

"Agents, actually. We're with the FBI," Rylie said as she looked at the girls. "Thanks for meeting with us. I understand you were friends with Vera Langley?"

Willa nodded. "Is it true? Was she murdered?"

Anne elbowed her.

"What?" she said, grabbing her side and wincing in pain. "I talked to Joe, who is buddies with George. He told his mom, who told Joe's mom. It's all over town."

Rylie waited for them to quiet down and said, "I need to know the last time each of you spoke with her."

The girls were quiet for a moment. Anne looked at Willa, who looked blankly at her nails. Anne was the first to speak. Her words came out shaky.

"I texted with her around seven o' clock last night."

"What about?" Rylie asked.

"Just talking about a date I was about to go on. Nothing much."

"What about you?" Michael asked Willa.

"Last time I spoke to her," Willa said, putting her nail file in her purse, "was two days ago. We went to lunch. We were in the parking lot, about to head home. She'd been talking about a conference she was going to in Pierre for her job. I said goodbye, and she got in her car and left."

"Did she seem okay when you saw her?"

114

Willa shrugged. "Same as always. I'm sorry...are you going to tell us what really happened to her? She was murdered, right? In our town?"

Rylie looked at Anne, ignoring the barrage of questions. "In the texts, did she seem like herself?"

"Yeah. What's...I don't understand. What's going on?"

This clearly wasn't going to end. And if the warning caused these girls to be more careful, then she'd rather they know.

"Yes. She was murdered," Rylie said bluntly. "Yes. She was smothered in her apartment last night."

The girls were silent. Anne's eyes glistened with tears. Willa's darted back and forth, as if she were expecting some other nasty surprise to come out of nowhere.

"So if you know of anyone who might have wanted to do her harm . . ." Rylie began.

"No," Anne said, wiping a tear from her eye. "I mean, I knew everyone she knew. She never talked about anything like that. Did someone follow her home from the conference?"

Rylie shrugged and looked to Michael to see if he had anything else to add. He cleared his throat. "If you think of anything, even the smallest thing, I want you to call me. Here's my card...just call." Michael pulled a stack of cards out of the inside pocket of his coat and handed one to each of the girls. "Also—"

Rylie's phone rang, interrupting him. She muted the ringer and checked the caller display. When she saw that it was coming from Kit, she gave everyone a quick glance and then stepped out of the restaurant area, lifting the phone to her ear.

"Rylie Wolf," she answered.

"Wolf, we've got some news," said the familiar voice of Kit, her voice strained.

Rylie's stomach dropped. "What is it, Kit?"

"Seems that the police have found a possible survivor of the killer you're looking for."

A flare of heat plummeted through her. If that was true, it meant the killer was really escalating, trying to claim more than one girl in a night. "Really? When did this happen?"

"I don't know. All I know is the survivor's scared as hell. They're trying to keep her at the Norvander police department headquarters, but

115

the father's creating a little bit of a stink, so I suggest you get on over there, asap."

Rylie and Michael headed towards the precinct in absolute silence. Now, one thing was sure: this was a sick son of a bitch who was getting sicker by the day.

Whoever he is, he's out of control, she thought, staring out the passenger side window, her thoughts flipping like a rolodex. Strangling? In the back seat of her car? That didn't sound right. The last time they'd mistakenly thought their killer had changed MO's, they'd learned it was another killer entirely.

The officer at the front desk was a fresh-faced kid of no more than twenty. The shiny silver nameplate on his chest said *J. Hawkins.* Michael showed him his credentials and said, "You have a crime victim we'd like to interview."

*

Twenty minutes later, Rylie was sitting behind a cheap folding table in the break room at the precinct, commandeering the room, as they sometimes did, to use it as a makeshift base of operations. Rylie was sitting in front of the pile of files on the victims, staring at the dry-erase board on the wall, trying to make sense of the information she had, when Michael walked in.

Alone.

She sighed. "Well, where is this girl?"

Michael held up a finger. "One minute. They're trying to soften her dad."

"Oh, I'll soften him," she said, clenching her hand into a fist. Apparently, her father was one of the overly protective types, which meant that he wanted to keep his daughter in bubble wrap rather than help catch the guy. "He's getting in the way of our investigation."

"Oh, I'm sure you would. You're like a regular meat mallet."

The room felt stale and smelled of coffee. Rylie rubbed at her head, trying to get some sort of thought process going. At this point, any ideas would be better than what they had . . . which was absolutely nothing.

She rummaged through the files and papers on the table, coming to the preliminary report on Vera Langley's autopsy. Because it was considered a murder case, the results had not yet been made public. In

116

fact, the coroner was being very insistent that the results he'd provided to the police were not complete. But the police had wanted something for reference, so the coroner had complied.

"You look at this yet?"

"I did. Nothing in it makes sense. Evidence of suffocation but nothing else."

Rylie nodded, letting out a sigh and shoving the coroner's report to the side. "I'm grasping at straws here. We need to talk to this victim."

"I know. Cool it. It'll happen."

She stared at the door, willing it to open. "Some things only happen if you make them happen. I don't care what this guy says. Tell the police to arrest him for obstructing justice. We need to talk to his daughter."

Michael leaned back in his chair and yawned. "Patience."

"Shit," Rylie said, slamming her hand down on the table. "I need a coffee. To hell with that. I need a beer."

But neither of them moved. They kept staring at the dry erase board and sifting through the piles of papers and documents without much enthusiasm. Meanwhile, phones rang outside and chatter continued at the front of the building. The calls had come with more frequency over the last hour. She'd been an agent long enough to know that the more crimes that went unsolved, the more calls the precinct would be fielding from worried citizens. They had every right to be concerned.

Finally, the door opened, and Officer Hawkins looked in. "Agent Brisbane? They're ready for you."

Michael smiled triumphantly as the officer led them down the hall to where the eighteen-year-old victim, Natalie Rouse, was waiting in an interrogation room with her father, Noah. The barrel-chested man with a beard and a scowl sat next to his daughter, arms crossed, looking as if he'd rather be anywhere else.

"This is obscene," he barked, his arm protectively around his pretty young daughter, who stared blankly into space. "They told me we could leave an hour ago. I thought we were done. My daughter's very tired and wants to go home."

"We're the FBI, and we think this might be part of a bigger case, a repeat offender, so we need to speak with her, too," Michael said, flashing his credentials. "You can understand that, considering we're doing everything we can to find this guy and make sure this doesn't happen to anyone else, right?"

117

Rylie was glad Michael was taking the lead on this. She would have already said something crude and inappropriate. The man cleared his throat self-importantly and checked his watch. "I've got to get moving. I have a meeting at—"

"This won't take long. Fifteen minutes or so. All right?"

He let out a sigh. "All right, but that's all. She's already been through the ringer. And you want to keep her here? She's fragile. Look at her. She's already made a statement. And she's the victim. Isn't this harassment?"

The girl was shaking, but that was understandable, after what she'd been through.

"It's not harassment if it can help someone else avoid the terrible situation your daughter was in," Rylie said, unable to help herself.

She would've probably gone further, but just then, Michael flashed her a warning look. *Enough.*

Just then, Natalie spoke up. "Dad! Dad, it's okay. I want to help."

An uneasy smile came over Michael face. He stroked his chin, waiting for the father's go-ahead. Rylie had to admire his technique, his calm demeanor.

Noah's defensive posture seemed to crumble. He let out a sigh and pulled his arm away from his daughter. "Fine. But I want to be present."

"That's perfectly fine," Michael said. "You can stay right there."

Natalie slumped in her chair, pulling her knees up to her chest. The first thing Rylie noticed were her nails—the French manicure was peeling, and the ends were bitten to the quick. She looked like a cat trapped between two dogs—somewhere between nervous and doomed. Her eyes were glassy, glistening with unshed tears.

"Hey, Natalie," Michael said, his gentle voice, as always, exactly what was called for in this moment. "Thanks for agreeing to speak with us."

"Just catch the guy. That's all I care about," she said, her voice trembling.

Natalie, in Rylie's opinion, was easily the prettiest of the victims. Dark-haired, with tawny skin and angular features, she had the look of a girl who'd blossom into one of those classic movie-star types in her twenties.

"Hopefully this won't take long," Michael said. "But Natalie, the more information you give us, the more helpful it will be in finding who did this."

She looked at her father and folded her arms over her chest, never making eye contact with either of the agents.

"Okay then," Michael said. "So just one more time. I want to hear what happened this afternoon. What you saw, what you did, what you said. Can you do that?"

She looked a little confused at first, then uncertain, her eyes darting nervously back and forth.

"I had just gotten off from work—I work at Derby Chicken, down the street. I forgot to lock the door to my car, I guess, before I went in for my shift. And so I got into my car and—"

"And she forgot to check the back seat. I'm always telling her to be careful, because someone could—"

"Dad," she muttered, rolling her eyes.

"Sorry," he said, looking down at his lap. "Go ahead."

"Anyway, I got into my car and pulled out, and then I noticed as I was driving, something in the rear-view mirror. Suddenly, some guy was choking me. He was wearing a—like, a ski mask. I scratched at his hands and screamed and he must've gotten scared, because the next thing I knew, he was running off, behind the restaurant."

"And that's it?" Rylie asked.

"Yes."

"Did anyone else see this happen?"

She shook her head. "No, it was between shifts. I was alone in the back of the lot. There was no one there. But as he was running away, he went to climb a fence and caught his pant leg on a part of it. I saw him tear open his leg. He must've really hurt himself because he limped off, toward the car wash next door."

"And you didn't get a description of him?" Michael asked.

"No, because of the mask," she said with a sigh. "He was short and stocky, though. And his breath smelled bad. That's all I know."

Michael nodded. "All right. Thanks for that information." He handed the father a card. "You guys are free to go. But if you think of anything else—"

Just then, the door swung open, and the officer in the reception area appeared, his face red. "Agents. I just got a call from one of our officers. He was calling around all the hospitals in the area and got a match. He's at the Minute Clinic on Wilton right now."

Rylie jumped up so quickly that the chair behind her flew back. "Let's go, Bris. Let's get this creep."

CHAPTER TWENTY TWO

The ride to the Minute Clinic took less than five minutes, but by the time Rylie burst through the double doors with Michael on her heels, a small group of doctors and nurses in various colored scrubs were standing in front of reception, worried looks on each of their faces.

"Are you FBI?" the only woman in a white coat asked. "We tried to get him to stay. But he got suspicious and took off that way."

"When?" Michael asked as Rylie's eyes frantically followed the doctor's pointed finger toward a busy main street.

"Not even a minute ago," Rylie heard the doctor say as she took off for him. When she reached the sidewalk, she saw a man with dark hair, in a black T-shirt, limping down the road, looking back at her.

In the next second he broke into a run, disappearing behind the line of trees.

"Bris! I see him!" she shouted, racing after him. She tore through the trees and found herself in what looked like a suite of professional offices. She saw him racing across the parking lot and slipping through another line of trees.

When she burst through the trees, she saw him, down an embankment, struggling to climb over a runoff ditch. As she reached for her sidearm and tried to take the decline as fast as she could, the gravel slipped and her feet came out from underneath her. Losing her grip on her gun, she fell onto her backside and started a long slide down the embankment.

Shit, shit, shit, she thought as pain sliced up her elbows. She tried to slow her slide, to grab for something, but there was nothing but gravel and broken cement. She didn't stop until she'd reached the bottom of the gulch, splashing her lower half into murky black water.

When she finally had her footing, she reached into the water, grabbed her gun, and tried to aim it at the man.

He was gone. "Shit!" she shouted aloud, splashing her hand down in the water.

Michael made it down the steep grade with the grace of an athlete. "You okay?"

"Fine," she sneered, feeling not just stupid, but uncomfortable, because now her clothes were full of wet mud.

"Where'd he go?"

"I don't know. That way," she pointed vaguely, jumping up. "Somewhere across there. He disappeared in the trees. You go right. I'll go left."

Michael took off. She was more careful this time as she dusted herself off and climbed the hill toward the tree line. When she stepped into the shade of the trees, the shadows played with the light filtering through the leaves, making it difficult to see. She tightened her grip on the gun, not wanting to part with it again, as she moved slowly through the forest, dead leaves crunching underfoot.

As soon as her eyes adjusted to the darkness, he darted out from behind a tree and took off, lumbering slowly with his injured leg clearly impeding his escape.

"FBI! Freeze!" she shouted, taking off for him when it was clear he had no intention of stopping.

When she reached the place she'd last seen him, she spun around, looking for him. Had he disappeared? After the earlier run through the cornfield, and the slide down the embankment, she'd just about had it. Her frustration mounting, she called out, "Bris! He's—"

Suddenly a form dove at her from the side, knocking her to the ground. The man was small but beefy, his biceps at least twice the size of her own. She fought up against him but he wrestled her to the ground, trying to pin her. He took both of her wrists, pressing them to the ground in effort to get her to drop her gun. But this time, she wouldn't let it go. When he tried to straddle her, his brow wrinkled, face contorting in hate, she bucked up, kicking him in the groin.

He let go immediately and staggered back, yelping like a wounded animal before collapsing among the exposed tree roots.

"*Ahhh,*" he screamed, clutching his privates as he writhed in pain. "What did you do that for?"

"I wonder," she sneered, reaching for her cuffs. She realized, too late, that she didn't have them, after their last criminal run-in. It was a rare day that they had to make two arrests. She leveled her gun at him and rolled her eyes. "Stop carrying on."

Luckily, though, the criminal was screaming so loud that a moment later, Michael came running through the trees, gun drawn. He shoved his gun in his holster and pulled out his own cuffs. "Good job, agent."

The compliment was little consolation to her as she looked down at herself. Exhausted, wet, and dirty, she looked like a drowned rat.

But at least, if they'd caught their man, she would feel glad about that.

*

After the police arrived to tote their latest suspect off, Michael grinned as they got into the truck. "Why are you upset? Because you're wet?"

"*No*," she said, though that was not really fun. She smelled like mold, and the drying mud felt tight on her skin.

"We should celebrate. We got the guy," Michael said as he took off, following the police cruiser toward headquarters.

She wondered if by "celebrate," he meant taking her out for dinner and drinks, that date. Even if he didn't mean that, it was premature. "Let's not break out the champagne until we've questioned the guy."

"It's him. Why else was he running away from us?"

"Because we're scary? The other guy was running away, too, remember?" she reminded him.

When they arrived at headquarters, Hawkins was at the front desk. "Thank God you're here. That guy won't shut up."

"Where is he?"

"In the detention cell in the back. He—"

Rylie raised a hand to quiet him and strode through the doors and down the long hallway, to the door to the two detention cells. The man was standing up, his fingers wrapped around the bars, scowling, and shouting at the officer there.

"Oh, good," the officer said, making himself scarce as quickly as possible.

The man's eyes were wild. They scraped over Rylie, disbelieving. "You're a detective? What kind of treatment is this? I didn't do nothing wrong. "

"I am FBI," she said, leaning against the wall opposite and folding her arms over his chest. "And you're in a load of trouble. What's your name?"

He pressed his lips together.

She tilted her head back and massaged her sore neck. So it was going to go like this.

123

Michael elbowed her and showed her the processing document. *Coby Forrester, 26, from Pierre, SD.* Well, that was something.

"Forrester. Did you assault a woman in her car in front of Derby Chicken?"

"No," he said, calming down slightly, avoiding their gaze. "I don't know anything about that."

"You don't? So you didn't try to strangle a woman?"

He pulled uselessly at the bars. "I don't . . . I don't remember."

"Hold on, hold on," Michael said, holding up a hand. He had the police report in his hand and was slowly paging through it. "You don't remember whether you strangled a woman or not?"

The man shook his head and muttered something under his breath that sounded like, *Forget it.* Then he pulled on the bars some more, his lips twisting sheepishly.

Rylie's eyes trailed down his beefy arms, and she understood. She reached out, grabbed his hand through the bars, and turned it over, bearing mottled skin, so ravaged by injection punctures and bruises that it looked like a minefield.

"He's an addict," Michael announced.

"Yeah," Rylie said, shaking her head, disappointed in herself. It was obvious to anyone, from his glassy eyes and haggard appearance, that he was on something. Why had it taken her so long to see? She'd been so blinded, looking for this killer, that she hadn't seen the signals, right in front of her.

He sniffled. "So what? I don't got anything on me. I didn't do anything wrong."

"Listen," she said, coming up close to him, so close that she smelled that awful breath of his. "We have a witness that saw you. And we know that you hurt your leg on that fence. So just tell us what happened before you're booked on murder charges."

He stared at her, the words not fully sinking in right away. A moment later, it seemed to hit him like a punch to the gut. "What? Murder?"

She expected absolute shock, just like that. Right then, she knew for certain that he wasn't their guy. Not only was the MO wrong, but no serious drug addict could commit a string of murders like that, leaving not a trace of evidence behind. But she still needed to find out why he'd attacked Natalie. "Tell us what you were doing in the parking lot of that restaurant."

He buried his face in his hands and said, "I guess . . . yeah. Now I remember. I needed money. Her car was open. I got in the back seat and was looking around for loose change. I swear, I didn't mean to hurt no one. But she got in and started to pull away. So I did the only thing I could think of. I didn't want to hurt her. When she screamed and stopped the car, I took off."

Rylie nodded. It was just as she'd thought. She glanced at Michael, who looked just as beaten as she felt. His eye was now completely swollen shut, and as he looked at her, he mouthed one word.

Dammit.

That was her thought, exactly.

"Let's go," she muttered, heading for the door.

CHAPTER TWENTY THREE

It was getting dark, the sun slipping lower and lower in the sky. Rylie watched it sink as they rode toward the hotel, her head tilted against the window. She felt like her mood was sinking along with it.

"So . . . dinner?" Michael asked.

She slowly turned her head to gaze at him. Was he serious? No, that was a stupid question. Of course he was serious. Food, to him, was no laughing matter. She looked down at her muddy clothes and said, "What makes you think that I'm in the mood to go out to eat?"

He hitched a shoulder. "All right. No problem. That's why we're going back to the hotel. We can shower up and then—"

"I won't be in the mood then, either."

He was silent for a moment. Then he said, "Okay, so do you want me to bring you something back?"

She scoffed. "Really, Bris? Is that all you ever think about? What I'm thinking about is that it's nearly nighttime. This guy has killed someone every night for the past three. He's going to strike again and we have no idea who he is. So I'm sorry if I don't have an appetite."

Her voice was getting more and more snarky as she went on, so by the time she was finished, she felt even worse. She didn't mean to rail on Michael, or to let her bad mood get to her, but she couldn't help it. Another woman might die tonight, and it was all because they hadn't been able to find this guy.

When the truck pulled into the lot at Motel Easy Rest, Michael cut the engine and looked at her. "Did you have any other ideas?"

She sighed. No, she didn't. And that was the problem.

He opened his door to get out, but she just sat there. Her eyes went to the room where poor Jessie Vega had been attacked, with the crime scene tape, stretched over the door, flapping in the breeze. She'd gone into that room, unsuspecting, just like another woman would be, tonight.

No. Rylie couldn't just go into her hotel room and have a pleasant night's sleep. Not knowing what danger was out there.

126

She needed to go somewhere and think. With absolute quiet, and without distractions.

Michael started to get out, but stopped when he realized she was rooted to her seat. "You going in?"

"I don't think I can," she said. "I have an idea. Do you mind if I take your truck and check it out."

He started to get back inside. "No problem, I'll come with—"

"No. I want to do it myself."

His eyes narrowed in suspicion as he studied her. She understood. They were partners. Anything regarding the case, they did it together.

She forced her tone to be lighter. "It's probably stupid. I don't want to waste your time. Just a hunch I have. You should stay here. That eye looks pretty bad."

He craned his neck to look in the rear-view mirror and winced. "Yeah. Okay, fine. I guess I can order take-out. Do you want me to order you some?"

"Yeah, that's great," she said.

She got out of the car and moved to the driver's side, where he was waiting. His expression was somber, and when he handed off the keys to her, he did so reluctantly. She could tell he was worried he might wind up regretting this.

"Don't worry. I'll be back in a half-hour or so," she said, getting into his seat and adjusting it to accommodate her smaller body.

"You'd better be. I'm coming after you, if not," he said, his voice fatherly.

She slammed the door closed, pulled out, and headed down the hill toward I-86, the Highway Thru Hell.

As she drove, she thought about how one could sense a coming doom. It was a prickle on her neck, and she felt it so strong now, she had to reach back there and rub it away. Still, it continued, as did the dread, pooling in her stomach, now that she knew that it meant nothing good.

Something's coming . . .

Rylie Wolf, nine, felt the back of her neck, prickling with sensation. It was a feeling she'd never experienced before, one that made her heart shudder in her chest.

She peered out the window. Sure enough, clouds were gathering in the wide Wyoming sky.

A storm. A storm was coming. She tried to massage the goosebumps away, but they only seemed to pop out more.

No, Rylie, worse than that.

She sat in the massive RV belonging to her neighbor, on one of the bunks beside the kitchen, watching Rose cook breakfast. The abundant sunshine framed her face, lighting up the flowered wallpaper and making everything bright and happy.

"You hungry, Ry?" Rose said, smiling up at her as she scraped scrambled eggs onto a plate. "Sleepy girl. You and Maren and Kiki must've stayed up way past your bedtime!"

Rylie laughed, rubbing her eyes, and looked around. "Where are they?"

Maren was her older sister, Kiki was Rose's daughter. They'd been neighbors, and fast friends—almost like family. Rylie and Kiki had done everything together, so that was why Rose had invited her and her mom and Maren on a "Girls Trip" in their family RV that summer, tooling about the campsites around Yellowstone. It had been so fun, on the road, like a dream—driving most of the day, hooking up at the campsite at night, drinking Cokes and margaritas while they sat by the fire and shared stories.

And then, in that one moment, everything had changed.

The always smiling, cherubic woman with the yellow curls looked to the window, and dropped the pan to the ground with a clatter. Hot oil spattered everywhere.

Suddenly, the clouds rolled overhead, casting dark shadows over the kitchen. Thunder boomed.

"Rylie," Rose warned, wiping her hands on her apron, and heading for the door. "Go to the back bedroom now."

She scampered down from the bunk and froze there. She'd always been told that the back bedroom was off-limits to kids. "But—"

"Do it! Now!" she shouted in a voice Rylie had never heard her use before.

More thunder boomed, and the earth shook with bright light, as if lightning had struck nearby. It spurred Rylie into action. Her skinny limbs working, she scrambled to the back of the RV and buried herself under the covers.

That was when she heard the rain, pattering against the metal roof of the RV.

Then, the crackle of thunder. Or were they gunshots?

Voices, then. Male. "I thought there were three?" one had said.
"Naw. Just those two."

And then the door had slammed, and after that, nothing.

Nothing for hours and hours. Or at least, it seemed like that. Rylie had been bathed in sweat by the time she'd pulled herself out from her hiding spot. She'd crept to the dirt-crusted window over the RV's kitchenette sink and stared out at the bodies, lying motionless in a circle. Kiki, Rose, and her mother. They'd all been shot, once, in the head.

But no Maren. Maren was gone.

Blinking away the images of her mother, best friend, and Rose, lying in a circle, their blood soaking the dirt floor of the RV park, she took a deep breath as she drove into the setting sun.

What did she know about this killer?

She knew he worked up and down this hellish highway. He could be in any one of the cars she passed, scouting out his next victim.

But how had he found them?

Rylie thought of the other killer, of the two women on the reservation. Marlon Greef. How had he found those girls, while working at that gas station in Sackville? He checked their IDs, and committed the address to memory.

Maybe that was how this killer operated, too. He got a look at their IDs, somehow.

Not Jessie, of course, since she'd stopped at a motel. But maybe she'd stopped there and asked him for directions to the nearest motel? At the Gas-o-Rama? But that place was crazy. There were so many people going in and out.

She drove faster, hitting a speed Michael had probably never taken the truck up to, deep in thought.

Clerks who sold alcohol would be able to look at IDs. Marie's route home from Wisconsin had taken her to the new Gas-o-Rama, as had Jessie's. But they hadn't purchased alcohol. And Vera hadn't stopped there. George had been adamant that she wouldn't have because she didn't like places like that.

So, then, where else had the killer gotten a look at their addresses?

She felt for sure that something had to do with the Gas-o-Rama, so she headed there. It was the next exit, and so crowded that she instead pulled into the parking lot across the street.

She watched it as so many people swarmed in and out, paying special attention to any men who looked suspicious. Most, though, seemed lost in their own world, getting their gas or whatever they needed from the convenience store and heading off in a matter of minutes.

Rylie shifted the seat back, took out her phone, and brought up the different files she had for the victims, to give them another look. As she paged through the photograph, she came to Marie Bottoms's driver's license, and stared at it until her vision blurred.

Did the killer see this? Is that why you're dead? Did he find out your address from this and follow you home?

She closed her eyes, thinking of Maren. It was scary how innocently crossing paths with a madman at the wrong time could derail a life so immensely. How many times had she wondered about that? Had they done something to attract Griffin Franklin's attention, and now her mother and friends were dead and Maren missing because of it?

When she opened her eyes, they caught on something.

Marie's drivers license's date of issue was only a week prior.

That was interesting. She opened up Jessie Vega's, and noticed the same thing. Her license had been renewed only two days prior to her death.

Her heart pounding, she opened up the file for Vera Langley, looking for her driver's license.

Her spirits deflated when she realized her license had been obtained as a teenager and hadn't been renewed in years.

But then she remembered something that Ed Barnes, the owner of TAYS-T pet food had said. *And I was looking for someone to handle my international accounts, which meant a lot of travel.*

Hadn't he said that TAYS-T operated in China and France? Which meant . . .

Quickly, she typed in "DMV near me" and waited for the search results to show up.

There was only one in this whole area of South Dakota, and it was in Pierre.

Not only did it offer license and motor vehicle services, but it also offered passports and passport renewals.

And it was located right off of I-86.

Bingo, she thought, throwing her phone on the passenger seat and shifting her car into drive.

CHAPTER TWENTY FOUR

When Rylie returned to the hotel, it was after eight, and the sun was almost gone. The cabins were all dark, except for a single light, glowing in Michael's front window.

She jumped out of his truck and took the steps to his cabin two at a time, but it wasn't fast enough for him.

He opened the door even before she got to it. She thought he'd be hunkered down for the night, but he hadn't even changed out of his rumpled jacket and slacks. In fact, he looked very much the same as she'd left him.

"You were an hour," he muttered, jabbing a finger at his wristwatch.

"Aw, were you worried about me?" she said, squeezing past him into the room. It smelled like fried chicken. Sure enough, there was a bucket on the table, an assortment of paper napkins, and two soft drinks, one full. He'd done as he'd promised.

"Getting there," he said, sitting down, picking up a half-eaten drumstick, and pointing to the food. "Dig in and tell me what happened. Did that big brain of yours come up with anything?"

"Maybe." She sat down, but didn't touch the food. She had something else on her mind. "I have an idea. But I need your help."

He chewed slowly. "All right. I'm listening."

She opened her phone and showed him the two photographs of the victims' licenses. "Notice anything?"

He picked up the phone and scrolled back and forth between them. "Other than them both being from South Dakota?"

She nodded. "Look at the renewal date."

He did, and one of his eyebrows cocked up, significantly higher than the other. "Okay . . . what about Langley's, though?"

"I don't know for sure, but remember how the owner at TAYS-T said she was going to be handling international accounts with a lot of travel?"

He nodded slowly. "So . . ." Before she could say more, his eyes lit up. "You think she might have applied for a passport there?"

Rylie nodded in excitement. "I checked. They do offer those services in this state, so it makes sense. And there's only one DMV in the area, so they must've all gone there."

"All right, all right," he said, grabbing his phone. He dialed a number and put it on speaker, then set it on the table, letting it ring between them. "It's worth a shot."

"Who are you calling?" she asked.

"Who else? Our one-man Geek Team."

The ringing stopped, followed by a click, and an unenthusiastic voice mumbled, "Yeah?"

Michael grinned. "Beaker. Stop playing video games. We need you."

"That's what I'm here for, boss," he said, becoming more alert. "What can I do you for?"

Rylie spoke up. "Hey, Beak. Can you look up employees from the Pierre South Dakota DMV for me?"

He scoffed. "Can a penguin fly?"

The two agents looked at each other with confusion. "Actually," Michael said, staring at the table, even as the sound of tapping keys filled the air. "I don't think a penguin can—"

"Done. Who wants it? You or Miss America?"

"Send it to both of us," Rylie said with a smile. "Thanks so much."

"All right. And it's off. I cross-referenced it with our criminal database so if any of them have any criminal records, it'll show up. Anything else?"

Michael shook his head. "Nope. That's it."

"Great. Next time, why don't you give me a hard one?" he muttered, and disconnected the call.

By the time she refreshed her email, it was already there, with no subject, since Beaker rarely used one when he sent them information. She opened it and began to scan the list of names. There were dozens of employees, listed in order of importance, from supervisors to desk clerks. Rylie scrolled through, finding little of interest. Most of the employees had squeaky clean records.

But then she came to one that had quite the history. Dennis Emory.

On his phone, Michael hit upon it at the same time. "Whoa, look at page seven."

"I'm looking," she said, scrolling through a couple of assault charges. There was also a note from a supervisor saying he'd been given a few warnings for using his position to steal personal information from customers. "He was fired. His last date of employment was . . . yesterday?"

She scrolled to the calendar on her phone to confirm, just as Michael said, "Hm. Looks like it."

"And he lives right outside of Pierre . . ." she said, inputting his address into her GPS. All her breath left her body as the app showed the route from the hotel to Dennis Emory's home.

He lived only three minutes away, off the same exit that they'd taken for the Easy Rest Motel.

She set the phone down in front of Michael, hoping he'd come to the same conclusion she had.

"We need to check this out," he said.

Yes. Her thoughts exactly. Heart racing, she grabbed her bag and patted her Glock. "Let's go."

*

When they pulled down the quiet, tree-lined street to the small ranch home, Rylie powered down the passenger's side window and squinted to take inventory of the surroundings. The lights in the house were off, except for a dim glowing from the front window.

Nothing unusual, and yet, a tendril of fear snaked its way up her spine. Something was off.

Before Michael could even throw the car into park, Rylie opened the door and jumped out onto the curb. She started to run across the street, but Michael held her back.

"Careful," he said, and she could tell by his face that he felt it, too. "Let me check it out first."

"If he's already after a girl, he won't be there, anyway. Every minute counts," she said, trying to rip her arm away from his, but he held her firm.

"But if he's our guy, and he *is* there, barreling in there without thinking will only get you more trouble," he hissed at her as they made their way to the front porch.

"We're just going to knock and be friendly," she said, with a shrug, but he gave her a look like, *Right.*

She knew he was right. As usual. Even when they tried to be friendly, they scared criminals off. They just *looked* like FBI agents, no matter what they did. And in not wanting another woman to suffer, she was being rash again, going off half-cocked.

Glowering, she crossed her arms and watched as he climbed the stairs and peeked into the window. "Do you see anything?" she whispered.

"Television's on, but I don't see anyone." He opened the front screen door slowly and silently, and knocked.

There was no answer, no movement from inside, so he knocked again, louder.

She nudged him out of the way and pounded. "Dennis Emory! This is FBI! Open up!"

On the last pound, the door shuddered. It was slightly open. She pushed again, and it gave way.

"Weird. If no one's home, why is the TV on, and why is the front door unlocked?"

They walked into the dimly lit home, and Rylie ran an eye over the living room, bathed in a blue light from the television. The couch was empty, but there was an imprint of a body on one of the cushions.

Someone had been there. Recently.

She opened her mouth to say something to Michael, when out of the corner of her eye, something flashed.

She looked past Michael in time to see a figure in the shadows, pointing a gun in their direction.

"Michael!" she screamed, grabbing him. He instinctively dove forward, throwing her behind the couch before reaching for the figure.

Stunned, she rolled over and yelped as a gun suddenly went off, taking a chunk of plaster out of the walls.

"Michael!" she shouted again as she heard the sound of their scuffling. She inched to where the two of them were fighting in the hallway, just in time to see Michael gaining the upper hand, wrestling the gun out of the assailant's hands. She rushed forward, grabbing her gun from the holster.

"Freeze!" she shouted, leveling it at him.

His eyes caught hers and he shuddered to a stop. He raised his hands over his head and peeled off Michael's body, then turned toward her, defeated. "This is a load of bullcrap," he muttered as Michael stood up and adjusted his tie.

Her partner looked okay, just a little flustered. "I'm sorry, what is bullcrap? You shooting at a couple of federal agents?"

"I didn't mean to. I didn't expect—I thought—I mean, I thought someone was breaking in," he said, breathing hard as he sat on the ground with his arms still raised. He was wearing a Minnesota Vikings T-shirt and loose tech shorts, his feet bare. The rest of him, though -- dark, gray-streaked hair falling in his face, scraggly beard, solid build-- gave him the look of a mountain man.

"We announced ourselves," Michael muttered, wiping the sweat from his face. "Or did you miss that part?"

"I did," he whined, blubbering. "I couldn't believe what I was hearing! I thought it was on the television. What are you even doing here?"

Rylie looked at the television, which was tuned to a crime show. She reached over, grabbed the remote from the sofa, and flipped it off. "Are you Dennis Emory?"

He nodded slowly.

"We need to question you in connection with a murder. You're coming with us."

CHAPTER TWENTY FIVE

By the time Rylie returned to the precinct, their newest suspect had already been processed and loaded into one of the two detention cells in the back. The place was starting to get crowded with their suspects— Coby Forrester, the drug addict who'd attacked his victim in the back of her car, was lying on one of the cots, in fetal position, facing away from them.

This time, though, she felt a little more confident that they'd gotten the right man.

Dennis Emory sat on the cot in the holding cell, his knees pulled up to his chest, his face buried in his arms.

As Michael came in behind her, he snapped his fingers. "Dude," he said, rattling the bars. "Come on. Look alive. We want to ask you some questions."

He looked over them with disinterest, then assumed his previous position.

Officer Hawkins opened up the cell. "Come on," he said to the suspect. "These agents want to ask you some questions."

Dennis Emory stood up and followed them out to the interrogation room, a smug look on his face. He looked like he was finding all of this funny.

Meanwhile, Michael and Rylie sat on the opposite side of the metal table, with his previous record. It was a doozy. Dennis Emory had faked his employment record in order to get his job at the DMV. He'd had a long list of previous crimes, ranging from passing bad checks to drug offenses to kidnapping and sexual assault. In fact, a lot of his crimes involved women. No fewer than three of his previous relationships, including an ex-wife, had filed restraining orders on him after domestic incidents. During one, he'd been arrested for attacking his wife with a knife, and when the police attempted to apprehend him, he'd nearly killed an officer.

Apparently, most recently, an employee at the DMV had tipped the powers that be off to the deception, and he'd not only been let go, but he was out on bail. awaiting trial for using his position in order to gain information on two women, who he'd followed home from the office and assaulted.

"So," Michael said, paging through some of his arrest records. "Dennis Emory. Let's start by you telling us where you were last night?"

He scraped his top teeth over his bottom lip and stared straight ahead, at a space on the wall between them.

Michael leaned forward. "How about when you got fired from your job at the DMV. What was that . . . yesterday?"

Again, Dennis Emory said nothing. He shifted his gaze to a different wall, as if the two agents weren't even there.

Rylie slammed a hand down on the metal table. "Emory. You're our lead suspect in a murder investigation. And if you don't want things to get really bad, really soon, you'd better start talking."

A sick smile spread over his thin lips, and he let out a low laugh. "I have nothing to say to you."

Michael leaned back and then reached into his jacket pocket and pulled out his phone. He produced the photograph of one of the women, Vera Langley. "You know her? We confirmed that she stopped into the DMV to get a passport while you were working there, and that you processed her application."

He looked at the photograph and shrugged, but Rylie saw something spark in his eyes.

There was definitely recognition in them. "You know her?" she prodded.

One of his shoulders went up. "Maybe. I don't know."

Michael stood up, leaning over the desk, assuming a threatening posture that made him look bigger than he was. "Do you," he spoke in a loud, calculating voice, "Or do you not know this woman?"

He sat back in his chair, amused.

Rylie gritted her teeth. Seemed like the more threatening they got, the more he enjoyed it. No, they needed to try another tack.

Michael pulled out the photograph of Jess Vega and showed him that one. "What about her?"

He licked his lips and grinned. "She's hot."

"Did you follow her home?" Michael said, even more frustration leaking into his voice.

The man simply shook his head.

"Don't bullshit me. I know my rights. And I won't say anything until I've got a lawyer here."

Michael threw up his hands. Rylie sighed and gave him the evil eye. "Fine. Stay here." She tugged on Michael's sleeve. "Can I talk to you outside?"

Michael continued to glare at the suspect, up until the moment they'd stepped out into the hall and closed the door. "Hawkins called. The public defender should be here in a few minutes. Then we can—"

"Bris."

Her voice was enough of a warning that he stopped. "Huh? If we can--"

Rylie said, "I don't know. Something's not adding up."

Michael's frustration, once focused on the spot where he'd last seen the suspect, now swung toward her. "What?"

"I don't know. I think he just seems wrong. Like he's not our guy."

"What are you talking about?"

Of course, he'd ask her to explain it, but right now, she wasn't sure she could. He was a dangerous felon, who'd been committing similar crimes to the ones he'd been apprehended for. She simply shrugged.

"No. Coby wasn't our guy. But this one checks out, Wolf," Michael said, pacing down the hall, his movements tight. He was beyond frustrated, and she couldn't blame him. Still, she couldn't stop the feeling. "Look. He was at the DMV with all of the victims. He has a history of assault."

"Assault," she said, opening up the file and showing the photograph of one of his victims, his ex-wife. She'd been beaten so badly, her eye looked almost as bad as Michael's did. Not to mention the bruising on her throat and her face. It was as if she'd been punched with his fist repeatedly. "Not suffocated. These victims were clean, except for that the killer held them down and suffocated them. They weren't beaten. It's nothing like this."

Michael studied it, hands on hips. She flipped to another one of his victims, a woman he'd taken home from a bar last year. She, too, had a black eye. Dennis Emory treated women like punching bags.

But this killer had not.

Finally, he let out a sigh. "He had the opportunity to follow all these women to their homes. Maybe this time, he was awaiting trial and he knew it would be bad for him if he was caught for any other crimes, and didn't want to leave his DNA everywhere."

"He didn't follow Jessie Vega to her home. He—"

"So? He followed her to the hotel. Same difference. He wanted to overpower them. It didn't matter how. He just wanted to have the control. That's what these guys want."

He stared at her, long and hard, with those piercing blue eyes. Those eyes could make her believe anything. And yet . . . she still wasn't sure about this.

She broke his gaze and her eyes trailed out toward the front of the precinct, toward the windows overlooking the parking lot. It was dark now. If Dennis wasn't their man, and the killer was still out there . . . he could've been prowling I-86 right now, looking for his next victim.

"Bris," she said softly, gnawing on her lower lip. "Can you handle things here for an hour?"

He crossed his arms tightly in front of himself and said, "Let me guess. You need to be alone and think."

"I just want to be sure." She gave him a pleading look.

He sighed and reached into his pocket, pulling out his keys. "You know, you're going to get yourself killed on one of these 'I-have-to-be-alone' thinking trips."

She snapped up the keys and spun for the door. "Thanks. I won't be long."

"One hour," he said, sounding very much like a strict father. "And make sure you answer your phone. If you're not back, I'm coming for you."

"You won't have to," she called to him, already halfway down the hall. When she stopped to peer over her shoulder for a split second, he was shaking his head doubtfully. She knew why. She'd gotten into scrapes, and he'd had to come after her before.

But this time, she couldn't ignore that gnawing feeling inside, telling her to dig deeper. She just needed to make sure and put her mind at ease.

CHAPTER TWENTY SIX

When she drove out onto I-86, heading east toward Pierre, Rylie was fighting for her second wind. It was after ten, she hadn't stopped to rest all day, and she was still wearing her mud-crusted clothes from her slip in the gully earlier, when they were chasing Coby the druggie.

The roads were almost empty, by this time of night. She cracked a window and let the cool air hit her face as she scanned the desolate road, hoping for a flash of wisdom. Her mind cycled over all of the evidence they'd compiled from the three murders, trying to pick out a stone that might've been left unturned.

They'd had Beaker pull the routes of the first two victims, based on cell phone records. But she hadn't yet asked him to do it for Vera Langley. That was something she could try.

She was so deep in thought that she didn't see the red brake lights ahead until she was practically on top of the car in front of her. Slamming on the brakes, she lurched forward. "What the . . ." she murmured, but then she saw the toll booth, up ahead.

Rooting around in the console, she managed to find a dollar, but the traffic up ahead didn't move. Probably someone who didn't have the money. This toll booth, way out in the middle of nowhere, was definitely messing with people.

"Pour soul," she murmured, reaching for her phone. And speaking of *messing*, she was probably messing up this case, making things more complicated than they needed to be. Michael was probably right—he usually was. If he had a hunch that Dennis Emory was their guy, then maybe she shouldn't have fought it. Maybe she should just go back to the hotel and get that rest she so desperately needed.

But still, something inside her was niggling, making that impossible. She'd never be able to rest unless she knew for sure.

Some impatient person up ahead laid on his horn, the blaring sound making her jump. It was kind of silly that they only had this one lane open. There was nothing to do but wait. Tapping her fingers impatiently on the steering wheel with one hand, she opened up a text to Beaker on her phone with the other, asking him if he could provide her with Vera Langley's route based on her cell phone records.

He responded right away:

Beaker: *You guys are boring me. Coming right up.*

She smiled and looked up. The traffic was starting to move again. A moment later, she handed over her dollar to the old lady at the booth and sped through the toll plaza.

Absently, she took off, wondering how long it would take Beaker to return that information. She checked her messages and it still hadn't arrived.

A text came in from Michael: *Everything okay?*

She was about to respond that it was when something hit her.

The toll booth.

If anyone knew the lay of I-86 in this section of the state, it was those toll booth operators. The overseers of the Highway thru Hell.

The thought excited her so much that she slammed on her brakes, causing another car behind her to lay on the horn and swerve around her. She navigated carefully to the left lane, found a police turnaround that cut across the grassy median, and took it.

Squealing out onto the westbound fast lane, she quickly gained speed, stopping at the toll booth on this side. There was no line going this way, and the operator was an African American male. "Hi," she said, fishing her credentials out of her pocket. "Special Agent Rylie Wolf, from the FBI. Is there a manager on duty I can talk to?"

"Sure." He motioned to the small brick building on the side of the road. "If you pull in there, you're going to want to talk to Olaf. He's the guy in charge."

"Thanks," she said, looking around for another dollar.

He waved her through. "No charge, ma'am."

"Appreciate it," she said, about to pull to the side, where a couple of cars were already parked along the shoulder of the road. "Hey. I have a question for you. Something I was just wondering."

He smiled. "What can I help you with, Agent?"

"When someone doesn't have the money, what do you do? You don't arrest them, do you?"

He laughed. "Sometimes I wish we did. Sometimes we get the same people, every day, who've got nothing but excuses." He lifted his mug of coffee and took a sip. "No, we just make them pull over, grab a copy of their driver's license, and then send them on their way. Then we mail them the bill in a week or so."

A copy of their driver's license.

The words echoed in her ears as she thanked him and parked along the side of the road. As she sat there, digesting this information, another big piece of the puzzle seemed to fit exactly into place: She realized that all the victims had passed through this toll booth on their way.

Every one of them. Even Jessie Vega, who'd only gone to the motel.

Grabbing her phone, she texted Michael: *I think I've got something. Emory might not be our man. But hold on. I'll know more in a bit.*

The shoulder of the road was narrow and dangerous; a big dump truck lumbered by, almost taking off her door as she opened it. She squeezed herself out and hurried into the brick building, to a lobby with a few tables and chairs, a vending machine, and signs pointing to restrooms down the hall. A man with a square, brown buzz cut and a goatee was working behind a desk, almost right in front of the door. Other than that, there was nobody else there. "Olaf?" she asked.

He nodded. "Are you applying for the toll collector job?"

"Already have one," she said, showing him her ID. "You're the manager here?"

He sighed. "Last time I checked. Too bad. We're really looking for a couple new bodies. No one's willing to work our hours, though. And I can't say it's the most fun job out there."

She nodded. As someone who never could stay in one place for too long, she couldn't imagine how toll collectors did it. "Can I ask you about your toll collectors?"

He laced his fingers together in front of him. "Of course. What do you want to know about them?"

"Could you get me a list of them?"

"Yeah. Former and current?"

"Mostly just current. Anyone who worked this past week. It would actually be helpful if I saw their schedules for the past week, too."

He pushed up close to his computer. "Yeah, sure. It'll be a short list, though. Like I said, I've been trying to fill a couple of open positions. That night shift is a real bear."

"I don't mind short," she said, leaning over his desk. *In fact, it'll be easier for me.*

143

He swiveled in his chair as the printer behind him came alive. "I'm printing it out for you. One sec." The machine hummed and spit out a paper, which he scooped into his hands and read over. "Here you go."

She scanned the list of six names. "These are all the toll collectors?"

"Yeah. Well, I do relief now and then, when I have to. You know, for bathroom breaks and things, whenever we're short." He sighed. "Like now."

From the list, she immediately zeroed in on the two men—Leroy Charles and Ralph Dickerson. They had local addresses. She studied their schedules and said, "Leroy Charles is . . ."

"He's out there right now. Good guy. You need to talk to him?" He reached for his phone. "I can bring him in and relieve him if you want?"

She shook her head. "In a minute, maybe. I see he normally works mornings?"

"That's right."

"And this other man, Ralph . . ." she started, scanning his schedule. "He works the—uh—"

"Evening shift. He gets off at one."

Rylie studied the schedule, making sense of it. He'd worked every night for the last three. Meaning, every night a woman had been murdered. "But he's not here now?"

The supervisor shook his head. "No, he's not. He actually just left. Said he had to leave early—wasn't feeling well."

She gleaned from the piece of paper in front of her a few things— one, that he'd been working there a few months. Two, that he always worked nights. And three, that he lived about ten miles east of the toll booth. But other than that, she knew nothing else. "What's he like?"

"Ralph?" He winced and blew out a heavy breath of air. "Well, he's kind of odd, to be honest. He's a good worker, that's for sure. But he's a little . . . strange. I don't know how else to say it."

"Has he ever given you a reason to worry about him?"

He burst out with a laugh, and then said, "Yeah. Actually. It's probably nothing. But he has a weird sense of humor. He's always talking about running people down when they can't pay. So I guess he's kind of dark. I don't think he'd go through with it, but . . . I think it's probably because of what happened to his wife." He paused, and then something must've occurred to him suddenly, because he said, "Hey. What is this all about? Is Ralph in trouble?"

She ignored the question. "I'm sorry. What happened to his wife?"

"She died. She was sick. He had to take some time off for that. I think he was really torn up by it. But other than that, you can set a watch to his schedule."

"That's terrible. Did you know what was wrong with her?"

He shook his head. "It was odd. She was sick for a long time, but she was getting better, he said. We asked how she was doing, and he said the doctor said she'd pull through. I never met her, but supposedly, she was very pretty. He was never specific about what, exactly, she had. And then the next thing I know, he tells me she died. I guess she had a relapse. He said something about how she couldn't get enough oxygen, and even the ventilator couldn't help her. At the end, she was just gasping for air. She was young, too. Only forty-five. Like him."

"He took it badly, then?"

"Yeah. Was out for a while. But when he came back, he seemed better. Just. .." He leaned forward as if about to tell her a secret. "Kind of a quiet guy. Not really one of the group."

She nodded, deeply in thought, thinking of something he'd said. *He said something about how she couldn't get enough oxygen.*

The more she played that sentence over in her head, the stranger it sounded. *Even the ventilator couldn't help her. At the end, she was just gasping for air.*

She looked at the address for Ralph Dickerson. Forty-two West Walton Street, in Sweeten.

"Do you happen to have the copies of the licenses he made today, for refusal to pay?"

The supervisor tilted his head and paused, as if trying to decide where they were kept. "Um, yeah, of course. I'll make you a copy right now."

He pressed a few buttons and the printer started to spit out paper. Tapping her fingers on the desk, she waited as about ten sheets came out. When Olaf flipped them over, she saw that each one had the black and white image of a driver's license. He stacked them, stapled them, and handed them to her. "Is there a problem?"

She shook her head as she looked through them. Immediately, she knew she could eliminate most of them. The men, and the older women. But there were still three young women in the group. Was one of them in danger?

"Thank you," she whispered, heading for the door. When she was back in the truck, her phone buzzed with a text from Michael, but she didn't bother reading it. Instead, she called him.

When he answered, she blurted excitedly, "It's not Dennis Emory. It's—"

"What? Rylie. We're about to book him on charges of—"

"Well, *stop*. It's not him. Just hold him there for a little longer."

"You know they can't keep him without charging him. His attorney's here."

"All right. Then fine. Tell them to charge him for that stunt he played when we came to his house. But not murder. He didn't do it, Bris."

"Just hold on a second and take a breath," he said, as if it was the easiest thing in the world. He was talking much too slowly for her liking. "Wolf. Who are you thinking—"

"It's Ralph Dickerson of 42 West Walton Street in Sweeten. I'm headed there now." Her words tumbled out as she started up the truck.

"Wait. The hell you are. Not alone. Pick me up first. Who is this guy? How do you know—"

"Just meet me there," she said hurriedly. "And I just know. Because Jessie Vega isn't even his first victim. I am pretty sure his wife was."

CHAPTER TWENTY SEVEN

Ralph Dickerson drove along I-86 toward a little town called Dupont.

He knew Dupont. It wasn't much of a place, right there on the outskirts of the Badlands National Park, but he knew it. It wasn't far from his hometown in Sweeten. It would be the perfect ending to the day. Once he got done paying Macey Polaski a little visit, he'd simply skirt on home, and be in bed by two.

He glanced at the photocopy he'd made of Macey Polaski's driver's license.

He had to smile. In the photo, she looked almost exactly like Virginia had, during her earliest years, when things were new and fresh between them. Blue-eyed and blush-cheeked, with honey-colored hair that curled around her face, she was like a picture, too beautiful to be real. And when she'd looked at him and her cheeks had blushed even redder? He was instantly in love.

Of course, things had soured, as they often did. He didn't like to think about that. He liked to remember how she was, before the mysterious illness gripped her.

It was an autoimmune disease, doctors said. They weren't quite sure how to classify it. It started as nothing, a few peeling patches of skin on her shoulders. A little cream, some oatmeal-based products, they said, would clear it up, like magic. But it didn't. Then it spread, up her neck, down her arms, over her torso, this horrible affliction of tissue-paper skin that cracked so easily, leaving massive crevasses in her skin, whenever she dared move.

So she didn't move. She stayed in bed, all the time. They had a nurse to help, at first full-time, then part-time, then once a day, until the money ran out. Then, it was left to him. At the last, she was nothing but a scaly white shell, like a wasp's nest, lined with deep, bleeding cracks all over her body.

And she'd become a bitch.

Oh, in some ways, he couldn't blame her. In their fifteen years of marriage, she'd gone from a gorgeous woman who turned every man's head, to a freak, some poor, decrepit thing that made people stare in disgust. She loved music, and singing, and playing the guitar, but she'd had to give up all of it. At the end, she found fault with everything, even him.

Especially him.

And he'd missed that old Virginia. Desperately. He nearly went mad, thinking of her, hoping that one day, she'd come back. Every day he spent with this new, terrible creature, the old Virginia seemed to get a little smaller, a little further away.

And he, too, had changed. He'd gone from fit and well, maybe not attractive, but normal—to a fat slob. After tending to her and enduring her taunts, his favorite thing to do was sit in front of the television and medicate himself with food. Until one day, he'd looked into the mirror, and he could barely recognize the Ralph Dickerson in front of him.

Finally, he'd had to put an end to it. Not just to her suffering, but to his own, as well. He'd crept up to her bed while she was sleeping, taken a pillow, and mercifully, ended it.

He remembered the way she struggled, and how the cracks had opened up in her skin, bleeding over her sheets, even as she fought for her life. But then, once he was done, and she was gone, as he pulled the pillow away, he was sure he saw a little of the old Virginia there.

His beautiful bride, the one who he'd fallen in love with, all those years ago. It was like she was back, and thanking him for alleviating her suffering. And for a moment, he was back, too—he wasn't that weird, fat, shy guy who repulsed everyone. Together, they were a couple that made people smile, the envy of many.

But that was a long time ago.

Now, it was everything he could do to keep that memory of his Virginia, his precious Virginia, alive in his head.

And this woman, Macey Polaski of Dupont, South Dakota, would help his Virginia live, just another day longer.

He thought of how frightened she'd been, when he walked over to her car after he'd told her to pull to the shoulder. She'd trembled, her hands fastened on the wheel with white knuckles, much like Virginia used to do whenever she was nervous. He'd asked her where she was headed, and she'd said that she was going home, to her apartment in Dupont. He'd asked her if she lived alone, and she'd nodded.

It had been so perfect that he simply couldn't have waited, even if he tried. So he'd told Olaf he felt ill, and of course, Olaf let him—his star employee—go home early.

Only, he wasn't planning on going home. Not just yet.

He had to stop at Dupont, first.

It was one in the morning by the time he took the exit for Dupont, leaving I-86 behind. He sped up, shifting his substantial backside on the seat of his blue compact car, excitement pulsing through his veins. *Soon,* he thought. *Soon I will bring you back, my dear Virginia.*

He'd plugged her address into his GPS, expecting the route would lead him to an apartment building. That's where these young girls usually lived. A condo, maybe. Jessie Vega, of course, had asked for hotel recommendations, and he'd told her a place not far from the toll booth, to make it easy on him. But most of the girls were just starting out, like he and Virginia had been in those early days, and so he expected a small apartment.

He was surprised when he pulled into a neighborhood with established, seventies-style split-level homes. The development was quiet and dark at this time of night, with only a dim streetlamp in front of each home. There was not a single sign of life, anywhere.

That was the way he liked it, but something made him pause. He couldn't imagine the Macey he'd seen, who'd gotten worked up over not having enough change to pay her toll, having the grit to purchase a home on her own.

But she *had* said she lived alone, and she seemed too sweet to be a liar. *She'd better not have lied to me,* he thought, gritting his teeth as the female voice on the GPS politely told him to turn left.

He did so, and when she announced that he'd arrived at his destination, the first thing he looked for as he pulled in front of a dark home was the Jeep.

He didn't see it anywhere. He saw a tilted mailbox and a WELCOME FRIENDS garden flag nestled among the landscaping, a long, empty driveway and a small, one-car garage. But no Jeep.

Maybe she pulled it into the garage, he thought, not giving up hope yet.

A few moments of surveying the home, and he made his plan. The yard was dark and lined with evergreen bushes. It was the perfect cover. He'd try to go in the back door.

He pulled around the corner and stepped out, checking both ways to make sure no one was watching.

Then he quietly made his way toward the house, walking slowly down the sidewalk. He made a quick left down the path to the back gate of the split-rail fence, easily undid the latch, and the gate swung open without so much as a creak. He pulled his substantial body through.

As he was about to go around back, he noticed the side door to the garage. It hadn't been part of his original plan, but it made sense. He went to it, twisting the knob, expecting to find it locked.

It wasn't. It opened. He pushed it open to total darkness.

Peering in, he could see nothing, so he reached around his giant backside to pull his phone out from his pocket, and opened the flashlight.

Before he could even turn it on, the glow from the phone's display confirmed his worst fears.

The truck wasn't there. *She'd said she was going straight home.*

The bitch had lied to him.

CHAPTER TWENTY EIGHT

When Rylie got to the house in Sweeten, despite driving ninety miles per hour the whole way, she already knew she was too late.

Not only was the place dark, but it was so eerily quiet, it seemed that no one had ever lived there before. There were no cars in the driveway, nothing to say anyone was home. Even the porch light was off.

But deep down, she'd suspected such a thing.

If she'd stopped to think and use her BAU training, instead of jumping on her first instinct, she would've come to the correct conclusion. This man, Ralph Dickerson, wouldn't be here. Of course not. He'd murdered three women in as many nights.

Now, he was out at his next victim's home, about to commit another murder.

The only question was, which one?

Michael wasn't there, yet, either. It made sense. He'd been all the way at headquarters, another fifteen minutes away, at the least. Knowing the way he drove, and that he'd probably have to commandeer a police car to make the trip, he'd probably take even longer than that.

She was on her own.

Quickly, she scanned the copies of the women's driver's licenses. Both were young and pretty, but it was Macey Polaski who stood out to Rylie the most. Macey lived in Dupont, which was the next exit off I-86. If Rylie gunned it, she could make it there in fifteen minutes, tops.

Making the decision, she quickly made a U-turn in the street and headed off for the highway. As she did, she put in a phone call to Michael.

"Hey," he said when he answered. "Almost there. Probably another five minutes."

"I'm not there anymore," she said, already bracing herself for his fatherly lecture about how she needed to be less impulsive. "Have the police go in and secure it. I think he might be taking his next victim in—"

"Wait. What? Stay right there."

"No. I can't wait. I'm going to Dupont. Her name is Macey Polaski and I think she's in—"

"Rylie!" he barked. "Listen to me. Don't—"

She ended the call and threw her phone down, already feeling the guilt seeping in. It was one thing to have Bill Matthews telling her to walk the line, because he didn't like anyone stepping on his toes, flouting his authority. But Michael Brisbane was coming from someplace totally different. He just wanted her safe.

He cared about her, and yet she couldn't extend him the same courtesy of caring about his feelings.

A woman's life was at stake. She only hoped he would understand that.

As she drove along the lonely stretch of highway, she pushed the limits of Michael's truck, forcing the speedometer to break 100. It still didn't feel like fast enough. Glancing at the photocopy of Macey's license, she realized that whoever had pulled her over had also taken down the woman's phone number.

Grabbing her phone, she dialed it with her thumb, bringing it to her ear. "Pick up," she mumbled. "Pick up!"

As if an answer to her prayers, there was a click, and a female voice said, "Hello?"

"Hi. Is this Macey? Macey Polaski?"

"Um, yeah. Who's this?"

Rylie sighed with relief. At the same time, she imagined the young girl, at home in Dupont, alone, a killer about to creep up behind her. "Listen to me. I'm Rylie Wolf with the FBI, and you're in danger."

She'd expected a "What?" or an "Oh, my God?" or even an, "Is this a prank call?" Something. Some sign of life. But there was nothing. Rylie heard the woman breathing on the other end, but nothing else.

"Hello?" she prompted.

The woman clucked her tongue, sounding annoyed. "I heard you. What is this? I don't understand."

She spoke louder, punctuating each word. "I'm from the FBI. My name is Rylie Wolf, and I'm tracking a killer. I believe you might be next. So I want you to stay put, lock your doors and windows, and I will be there in a—"

"Look. I don't know who you are," she said with a hint of disgust in her voice. "But I'm not playing along anymore. Goodbye."

"Wait!" Rylie shouted, incredulous. "Wait! Macey!"

"What?" she snapped.

"I'm telling you, this is no joke. Just lock your doors and windows and I will be there in five minutes. Do you understand me?"

There was a rush of air. "Whatever. Look, I'm not even at home now. Like I told the FBI agent the first time you called, I'm at my uncle's place, babysitting my cousins."

She stiffened. She wasn't at home? "The first time . . .?" she began. "Someone called you before?"

"Yeah," the girl said. "And gave the same crap about how I was in danger and asked where I was. If you're going to try to play games with me, at least get your stories straight."

Rylie blanched. She hadn't gone home, which was the only reason she was alive right now. If she had, Ralph Dickerson would've gotten to her by now. He'd called her, on a hunting expedition, pretending to be the FBI. And now he had a head start.

"Give me that address," she said, pushing hard on the gas as the exit for Dupont came into view. "Now."

"But— why should I?" Uncertainty made her voice quiver.

"Because you're in danger, and the person who called you before might already be there to do you harm."

"One-twenty-six Pembroke Lane in Dupont," she said, her voice finally cracking with uncertainty. "Wait . . . what's going on?"

"Macey. Listen to me. Lock your windows and doors and hide. Do not come out until you hear my name. Okay?"

"Uh, okay . . ." she said. "I'm going."

"Stay on the phone with me," she said as she tore off to the right, for the exit for Dupont. She set the phone down in the cup-holder and plugged in the address for Pembroke Lane. Once she did, she grabbed the phone. "Macey?"

Nothing.

"Macey?" she said louder, in a panic, now.

She threw the phone down, frantic, as she reached the bottom of the ramp. There was a red light there, but she soared through it, chasing the directions on the GPS. The voice on it couldn't keep up with her speed. The ETA said three minutes.

In three minutes, Macey Polaski could be dead.

153

CHAPTER TWENTY NINE

Rylie made it to Macey's uncle's home on Pembroke in less than a minute. She slammed on the brakes and jumped out of the truck, rushing for the front door of the double-wide trailer home. As she did, she grabbed for her gun. Unlike the other home, a couple of windows were awash in light, and she could see movement beyond. When she reached the front door, her heart leapt into her throat.

The door was open.

Rylie crouched by the steps to the trailer, trying to decide what to do. Whatever it was, she had to do it fast. Michael and the police would be here soon, but not soon enough. She had to act.

Pressing her body against the side of the trailer, she crept up the steps, one by one, until she could peel her head away and peer inside. She saw a body of a man, lying on the floor, motionless. Changing position, she looked through the nearest window, through the slanted blinds. From there, she could see a woman, Macey, her face rigid with fear. Someone was standing in the room with her, but she couldn't see who.

Thank God. She didn't know who was on the ground, but at least Macey was okay. Still, she knew there wasn't much time.

She climbed up the final stair and ventured another look inside, her blood boiling as she saw a large man come right up to Macey, who pressed herself up against the wall, trembling in fear.

Rylie watched as he brought the pillow up to Macey's face and whispered in her ear as she winced against the wall. In the reflection of the window, Rylie saw a patrol car speeding down the street, toward her. She waved to the car silently, took a deep breath, and burst inside.

"FBI! Drop—"

She couldn't quite register how it happened, but an arm came out of nowhere, knocking her to the side, against a wall. Her vision wavered as her head smashed into it. It didn't make sense. From the window, she'd seen him, across the room, about to smother that poor victim, but now, she could feel his enormous form behind her, reaching for the gun in her hand as he wrenched her arm behind her.

154

The only thing she could do was scrape her hand back, shoving uselessly at him as his huge body pressed her up against the wall. "This has nothing to do with you, bitch," he muttered.

With all her strength, she shoved an elbow into his breastbone.

He coughed, but only let go slightly. It was enough, allowing her to spin, enough to see Macey, staring wide-eyed, across the room, but not enough for her to aim the gun at him. He came for her again, and she reached her free hand out, fastening it around his fleshy neck.

She slowly loosened her grip on his neck, waiting . . . waiting . . . for the right moment.

Then, with everything she could, she jammed her forearm into his throat.

He let out a guttural sound and clutched at his neck.

"Ugh!" He staggered back, and she followed her Quantico self-defense teaching with another jab to his solar plexus, right in the center of his chest. As he lunged forward, she kneed him in the groin and dug her fingers into his eyes, scratching at his face.

The rest happened so fast. As he doubled over, reaching out blindly, wildly for her, she skirted away and raised the gun. "Freeze."

A thrill of adrenaline surged through her as she breathed out the word, "Freeze, Dickerson."

"BITCH!" Dickerson roared, his breath coming out as rasps. He had a bloody scratch from her fingernail near his nose.

He wiped at it, and at the sweat on his forehead, then studied the blood on his fingers, as if hardly able to believe she'd hurt him.

Rylie thought that was it. That he would submit when faced with her gun. But she was wrong. Before she knew what he was doing, he lashed out wildly at her, cracking the back of his hand across her face.

She saw stars from the impact as she wavered on her feet, finally staggering backwards, against the wall. She brought her hand to her jaw and tasted the metallic tang of blood on her tongue.

It was in that delirium that she barely realized that she no longer had a grip on her gun.

Through double vision, she saw him in front of her. No, *he* had her gun.

He stalked toward her and drove the barrel of the gun into the top of her head, shoving her to her knees. She squeezed her eyes closed and waited for the gunshot, for the world to go black.

155

But then, she felt the air of a door, bursting open. After that, a buzz of chaos. Everything happening in flashes. Her mind reeling, she couldn't quite see or think. A voice shouting. The ground under her vibrating. The sound of a scuffle, and a gun clattering across the floor. More shouts. Someone's fist connected with her jaw, knocking her flat on the ground.

When she opened her eyes, she found herself lying on her back, her head tilted to the side, chin touching her shoulder. She saw the gun on the floor. She wanted to lunge for it, but she had no energy left. Blood rushing through her ears, she watched as someone else got there first.

Her vision swimming, she closed her eyes. Again, she expected the gunshot, so when it happened, this time, she wasn't the least bit surprised.

What did surprise her was that there was no pain. None at all.

There was only the sound of something slumping to the ground, beside her.

And when she finally dared to open her eyes, Ralph Dickerson was lying there, dead, a splotch of blood spreading across his chest.

"Rylie?"

She blinked hard and tilted her head up to the sound, and saw Michael's face hovering over her, just inches away. His hand was on her cheek, his eyes full of concern. "What . . .?"

"Don't worry about that," he said, but she knew. He'd come in just at the right time, as usual, and shot Ralph Dickerson dead. "Are you okay?"

She lifted her head up an inch, and found the pain wasn't so bad. So without even thinking too much about it, in a haze of adrenaline and relief, she lifted up the rest of the way and planted a kiss on his lips.

EPILOGUE

The following morning, with another case finally solved, Rylie and Michael started the two and a half hour ride back to Rapid City. The ride home was mostly silent. It was strange to think that Michael, the chatty person he was from the moment they'd met, was getting less and less talkative, as their time as partners wore on. She found herself missing his nonstop stream of consciousness chatter. There was a certain tension in the cabin, and she had a feeling she was the one who created it.

So she was happy when he lowered the volume on the radio, cleared his throat and prepared to speak.

But then he asked her something that she wished he wouldn't have. "What are you thinking about?"

She shrugged nonchalantly. "Nothing."

"Are you sure? Seems like you have something on your mind?"

"Oh," she said, finally coming up with something to say. "I was thinking about Ralph. It's kind of sad. I guess I feel bad for him, in a way."

He let out a short laugh. "Seriously? Because he murdered those girls? And almost killed *you*?"

"No," she said quickly. "But because they were probably in love, and then she got sick, and he lost his mind. It's strange how things like that can happen, how life can turn on a dime."

Which reminded her . . .

She grabbed her phone and opened it, realizing she had a message from Kit. *Good work out there. BTW, your appointment request has been granted. Thursday at 11 am.*

She swallowed. That was only two days from now.

Two days, and she might come face-to-face with the man who took her sister and sent her life spinning.

"Very profound," he said, looking over at her. "Anything else on your mind?"

He was fishing for something. She knew exactly what, but she wasn't going to say it. Not out loud. She'd die first. It was better to wait for him to say something.

So instead, she said, "No."

"That Kit?" He was staring at her phone.

She quickly shoved it in her pocket and said, "Yep. Just wanted to know when we'd be in."

"Geez. You'd think she'd give us a break, considering we kicked ass and took names yesterday. Huh?"

She nodded, facing out the window, imagining coming face-to-face with Griffin Franklin. She'd never been inside this prison before. This, she felt, had the potential to be the most important meeting of her life.

"Hello?"

She turned back and realized that Michael had said something to her. "I'm sorry, what?"

"I just asked if . . . well . . ." He reached up and rubbed the back of his neck, something he only did when he was nervous. "If you remembered what you did last night. After I shot Dickerson?"

He was trying to play it off coolly, but she couldn't help feeling like he looked like a middle-school kid, asking his crush to the dance. Awkward . . . but absolutely endearing. She shook off thoughts of Griffin Franklin and smiled. "I kissed you."

He seemed delighted that she remembered it. "Uh . . . yeah. What was that all about? Did you . . .think I was someone else? Hit your head too hard?"

She laughed. "No. I knew it was you, Bris. I just . . . have no idea why I did it. I guess it was the adrenaline."

"Oh," he said, nodding. "Right. I can see that. I mean, that's why I kissed you back. The adrenaline."

They stared straight ahead for a while, and it felt like they were in a contest to see who would speak first. Finally, she said, "We should go out for dinner. You know, now that the case is over and everything. So I can show you that I know how to relax and have a good time."

He smiled. "Yeah. My thoughts exactly. Friday night?"

"Yep," she said, settling back in her seat. "Friday night is perfect."

*

On Thursday morning, before the sun and most of the residents of her apartment complex had risen, Rylie got into her own truck and took off on the highway, heading north. But it was only when she crossed the border into North Dakota, passing a giant yellow sign that said PRISON AREA DO NOT PICK UP HITCHHIKERS, that her stomach began to somersault.

A moment later, a hulking cement structure grew out from the chocolate-colored mountains, the curled barbs of concertina wire from the peripheral fence glistening in the sun. After that, an imposing gate. She stopped at the gate and yawned, trying to be casual, even though her nerves were buzzing.

The guard's smile when she showed her ID did nothing to help her. He did a perfunctory search of the car and waved her in through a solid steel gate. Her heart, which had already been throbbing when the truck left Rapid City, felt like it was in its own prison, pounding on her chest wall, trying to escape. She'd eaten a banana before she left, hoping it would settle her stomach, but as she was admitted beyond the prison gate, she became very certain that she was going to lose it.

She swallowed the vomit gurgling in the back of her throat, but it did no good. Slamming on the brakes, she powered down the window and painted the pavement with a watery, colorless substance.

Embarrassed, she tried to demurely wipe her mouth with a tissue, and continued down the road.

Girl, she thought to herself sourly, trying to calm her breathing, *if you were wound any tighter you'd be broke.*

She rustled through her bag and popped a piece of gum. Then she turned into the parking lot.

When she stepped outside, though it was a warm day, she shivered. The air was deadly still as she crossed the lot, heavy with the pungent stench of rotting trash. She stepped into a long cinderblock hallway that slanted down, as if descending straight into hell, though the air was at least forty degrees cooler than outside. She rubbed the gooseflesh from her arms and followed the signs toward the entry.

The guard, a middle-aged woman with a triple-chin and thick glasses, looked at her expectantly. She cleared her throat. "Rylie Wolf from the FBI. I have an appointment to see Griffin Franklin."

She frowned and gruffly asked for two forms of identification. She furnished her license and credentials. After taking down her

159

information, the guard made a quick telephone call. When she hung up, she said, "You're going to have to be screened."

Rylie frowned. "I'm FBI."

She looked at Rylie, a *Listen honey, you don't know who you're dealing with* expression on her face. "These are the rules. Come along."

She opened a door to a dark room that looked like a dungeon. Rylie's eyes lost focus, and everything turned gray in the blur. Her useless eyes found the clinical linoleum on the floor, which was undulating under her feet. Either it was an earthquake or her knees had just turned to goo. Her voice squeaked, "Okay," and she made herself move, feeling as if she was about to throw herself into a volcano as sacrifice.

A torrent of fear was building inside her chest, wracking her body with small, strange, uncontrollable spasms. She couldn't hold her phone; it kept slipping from her shaking hands. Her upper lip twitched, like Elvis's. She blinked to try to focus, her eyelids fluttering like a child's flipbook. It was truly a frightening moment. The guard spoke mechanically, undeterred by her little fear dance as she escorted Rylie through the door. "You are going to meet with Mr. Franklin in the white room. Ordinarily you'd meet with prisoners in the booths, but Franklin is a special case. Step this way."

Special case. She didn't need to know what that meant. She already understood.

Griffin Franklin was the worst of the worst.

The guard ushered Rylie through a metal detector. It buzzed. She produced a detector wand and waved it over her body, beginning with her feet. When she reached chest-level, it buzzed again. "Are you wearing underwire?"

Her question caught Rylie off-guard. She was finally concentrating on the breathing exercises she'd learned for stressful situations in Quantico, as she had never needed them so badly. The guard stared at her, confused.

Exhaling loudly, she said, "Possibly. I guess so."

"You'll need to remove your bra before entering, then." She pointed to the ladies' room.

Stunned, Rylie retreated into a stall and removed her bra, feeling odd. *Of course, no smart person would bring an underwire bra into prison! How could I have been so stupid?* She rolled it up and stuffed it into her handbag.

Shuddering at the thought of meeting her sister's kidnapper, Rylie tried to arrange her flimsy silk jacket so it wouldn't lie so perfectly against her contours, but it was no use. Crossing her arms in front of her chest, she skulked into the lobby with all the presence and confidence of a deflated balloon. "Ready."

The guard proceeded to scan her body with the wand. This time, she was clean. She reached over and took Rylie purse. "Have anything in here you'd like to bring with you?"

"What's allowed?"

"Tissues, a handkerchief." The list ended very abruptly.

"Can I bring my pad and pen to take notes?"

"No. No pen. Sorry."

"But—to take notes?" She held up the pen and paper she'd brought.

"I will have to take a look at them." She dissembled the pen and flipped carefully through the notepad, then handed them back to her. "Okay. You'll have one hour. You will be in the room with the prisoner and a guard; there will be another two right outside the room. I urge you not to move out of your chair once you are seated. If you need anything, let a guard know.

"You are not permitted to touch or give anything to the prisoner. You may speak to him, and that is all. I wouldn't move too much. All right?"

Rylie nodded.

She picked up the phone and dialed a number. Another guard arrived and asked Rylie to follow. She clutched the notebook against her chest to hide it and walked dutifully behind her leader, through two sets of security doors. Finally, they stopped, and he pressed his identification into a keypad. The door swung open, revealing a simple table, separating two chairs.

"Sit down on the chair facing us," the guard instructed. "The prisoner will be here in a minute."

She lowered her body down cautiously, her bare forearms shocked by the cold metal of the chair. It was hard and was likely to begin to feel uncomfortable after a full hour, but she knew that she would have much more important things to occupy her mind in a moment. Opening up her notebook, she scanned the questions she had prepared. *Can I really ask these? Will my mouth even open and allow me to get the words out?*

161

She stared at the wall. There was nothing really to see there, only some chipping paint on the cinderblock, and a cobweb or two in the far corner. The door was just as nondescript; it didn't even have a window. The room, as small as her cubicle at work, was too small, too confining. Even from the moment she had entered the facility, the air took on a heavy, sickly quality, almost as if there wasn't enough oxygen to go around. Rylie inhaled deeply, knowing she would never be able to be a prisoner.

Five minutes passed, then ten. The door eventually became the sole object of her concentration; soon, it would open, and she would be in that tiny room with a man who had ended the lives of numerous women. She convinced herself to stare at her notes, since counting down the seconds until she greeted the man was slowly driving her insane. But her notes were just a jumble. *How can I ask any of these questions? I can barely read them.*

When the hinges finally did creak, the three guards stepped in, two escorting the murderer. The doorway was filled with a hulking figure, who bowed his head to enter. He stood two heads above the tallest guard. The short-sleeved, orange jumpsuit revealed his hairy, muscle-bound arms. In contrast, his head and eyebrows were completely clean-shaven. Very prominent on the smooth, white skin of his neck, was a ruby slice, stretching from his jaw line to collarbone.

But it was the eyes that hit Rylie right away—those empty, round shark eyes, black and mysterious as the night. They were focused right on her.

She looked away, which was all she could do at the moment. She felt a bead of sweat run from her underarm, past her ribs. When her reluctant gaze returned, he was seated in his chair, table pulled up to his massive chest. He was still staring at her.

This time, smirking.

"Hel—" her voice cracked on the very first syllable.

Good start. Just perfect.

She took a breath and started again. "Hello, Mr. Franklin. My name is Rylie Wolf, and I'm a Special Agent with the FBI. I asked to meet with you so that I can ask you a few questions."

His grin widened but his hands remained still. She silently cursed her stupidity. She wasn't there to dance with him or play Parcheesi. *Obviously* she wanted to ask him questions.

Forcing her voice to be calm, she said, "My first question is—"

He grunted like an ox, and said, in a voice so gruff and gravelly that it rumbled across her eardrums, "What is your name, dear?"

He tilted his head, gazing at her in an unsettling way that made her think he was peering deep inside her soul.

She paused. She'd come here to unravel his secrets. She didn't want *him* doing the same to her.

And yet, she got the feeling that was exactly what he was doing. His thick elbows on the table, he pressed the fingertips of both hands together in front of him, waiting.

She felt trapped. She could do nothing but answer.

"Rylie Wolf from the FBI," she repeated in a louder voice, enunciating as if talking to a partially deaf person. She decided she'd have to speak a lot slower. At this rate, they'd only have cleared up the most basic facts by the end of the one-hour period. "I wanted to find out—"

He grunted again so loudly it nearly drowned out her voice.

"Where are you from, dear?"

She stared at him, that same, unsettling stare squeezing her heart, her lungs, everything inside her. She managed to sigh in exasperation. "Mr. Franklin. Please. I'm asking the questions here."

He balled his hands tightly into fists, eyes closed as if in prayer, and then resumed.

"How old are you, dear?"

This was intolerable. She looked at a guard for help, but he stared back at her with a shrug that said, *You asked for this.* "Mr. Franklin, I have a lot of questions to ask, and not much time, so do you mind if we get started?"

He grunted and crossed his enormous arms in front of his chest.

"Thirty-five," she finally answered. "Now, may we continue?"

He nodded, satisfied, and the smirk widened.

Every single hair on the back of Rylie's neck stood at attention, and a strange, overwhelming sense of déjà vu enveloped her. She opened her mouth to speak, but no word, no sound came out. Her vocal cords had frozen.

She couldn't fight the feeling that he knew exactly who she was, and why she was there.

Almost as if reading her mind, he said, "You know, dear, I believe we have met, once before."

DARE YOU
(A Rylie Wolf FBI Suspense Thriller—Book 6)

On a stretch of highway in the Pacific Northwest known for the country's highest number of serial killers, cold cases pile up across state lines, stumping the local police. An elite FBI unit is formed, with brilliant special agent Rylie Wolf at its head—and Rylie is summoned urgently to a region where unsuspecting accidents have converged with murders. Can she find the link?

"Molly Black has written a taut thriller that will keep you on the edge of your seat... I absolutely loved this book and can't wait to read the next book in the series!"
—Reader review for Girl One: Murder

A complex psychological crime thriller full of twists and turns and packed with heart-pounding suspense, the RYLIE WOLF mystery series will make you fall in love with a brilliant new female protagonist and keep you turning pages late into the night. It is a perfect addition for fans of Robert Dugoni, Rachel Caine, Melinda Leigh or Mary Burton.

Future books in the series will be available soon.

"I binge read this book. It hooked me in and didn't stop till the last few pages... I look forward to reading more!"
—Reader review for Found You

"I loved this book! Fast-paced plot, great characters and interesting insights into investigating cold cases. I can't wait to read the next book!"
—Reader review for Girl One: Murder

"Very good book... You will feel like you are right there looking for the kidnapper! I know I will be reading more in this series!"
—Reader review for Girl One: Murder

"This is a very well written book and holds your interest from page 1... Definitely looking forward to reading the next one in the series, and hopefully others as well!"
—Reader review for Girl One: Murder

"Wow, I cannot wait for the next in this series. Starts with a bang and just keeps going."
—Reader review for Girl One: Murder

"Well written book with a great plot, one that will keep you up at night. A page turner!"
—Reader review for Girl One: Murder

"A great suspense that keeps you reading... can't wait for the next in this series!"
—Reader review for Found You

"Sooo soo good! There are a few unforeseen twists... I binge read this like I binge watch Netflix. It just sucks you in."
—Reader review for Found You

Molly Black

Bestselling author Molly Black is author of the MAYA GRAY FBI suspense thriller series, comprising nine books (and counting); of the RYLIE WOLF FBI suspense thriller series, comprising six books (and counting); of the TAYLOR SAGE FBI suspense thriller series, comprising six books (and counting); and of the KATIE WINTER FBI suspense thriller series, comprising eleven books (and counting).

An avid reader and lifelong fan of the mystery and thriller genres, Molly loves to hear from you, so please feel free to visit www.mollyblackauthor.com to learn more and stay in touch.

BOOKS BY MOLLY BLACK

MAYA GRAY MYSTERY SERIES
GIRL ONE: MURDER (Book #1)
GIRL TWO: TAKEN (Book #2)
GIRL THREE: TRAPPED (Book #3)
GIRL FOUR: LURED (Book #4)
GIRL FIVE: BOUND (Book #5)
GIRL SIX: FORSAKEN (Book #6)
GIRL SEVEN: CRAVED (Book #7)
GIRL EIGHT: HUNTED (Book #8)
GIRL NINE: GONE (Book #9)

RYLIE WOLF FBI SUSPENSE THRILLER
FOUND YOU (Book #1)
CAUGHT YOU (Book #2)
SEE YOU (Book #3)
WANT YOU (Book #4)
TAKE YOU (Book #5)
DARE YOU (Book #6)

TAYLOR SAGE FBI SUSPENSE THRILLER
DON'T LOOK (Book #1)
DON'T BREATHE (Book #2)
DON'T RUN (Book #3)
DON'T FLINCH (Book #4)
DON'T REMEMBER (Book #5)
DON'T TELL (Book #6)

KATIE WINTER FBI SUSPENSE THRILLER
SAVE ME (Book #1)
REACH ME (Book #2)
HIDE ME (Book #3)
BELIEVE ME (Book #4)
HELP ME (Book #5)

Made in the USA
Monee, IL
27 August 2024

64674899R00102